PARADISE

ZONE CYBORGS BOOK 2

JESSICA MARTING

SHADOW PRESS

PARADISE

CONTENT WARNING:

This book contains discussion of abuse, drug use, addiction, and kidnapping.

For David

CHAPTER 1

MATTHIAS HAD BEEN on the receiving end of life-altering bad news quite a few times in his thirty-three years: the death of his father. The death of Barney, his dog. Being deployed to the Brava System twice for a war that hadn't made any sense then and still didn't. The recently revised tax structure levied on independent freighter operators. But he'd never quite felt like he'd been sucker-punched in the gut by words until Marielle—the woman he was more than fond of—said what he never expected to hear.

"You want to break up," he said flatly. His voice was nearly drowned out by the noisy wheels of cargo bots. They scraped over the hangar's grimy floor as they unpacked crates of replicator nutrition components from his third-hand freighter's hold. The *Ensign*'s paint job was starting to peel off in places, but she was still a reliable vessel. The *only* reliable thing in his life, apparently.

Marielle fiddled with the ends of her long blond hair, not meeting his gaze. "Look, we want different things in life," she said. "It's for the best that we cut this thing off before anyone gets hurt."

"*I'm* hurt," Matthias said. "I care about you."

A flash of something he didn't recognize flitted across Marielle's face. Disgust? Mockery? He couldn't tell. It was gone just as quickly, her features schooled into a neutral expression. "Please don't say that," she said. She squared her shoulders, and her gaze finally met his. "I think it would be best if you steered clear of Antonoff Station for a while. Can you do that?"

Matthias's hurt was temporarily replaced by anger and awe. "Are you insane? Of course not." Antonoff Station was the largest and cheapest commercial hub in Zone space. It was where he picked up most of his shipping contracts, where pretty much every freelance freighter operator picked them up. It was career suicide to sever his connections with Antonoff, even temporarily.

Marielle actually had the audacity to look pissed off at that statement. "Look, I just don't think you being here would be good," she said, her voice rising in volume. "I lived here long before you showed up. It's *my* station."

Was she drunk? "It's a Zone station," he said. "It belongs to everyone."

He realized the stupidity of his words as soon as he said them. Antonoff Station might technically be public property, paid for by the ever-increasing taxes levied on Zone citizens, but it was run by private interests who didn't give a shit about the average person as long as they could keep their paws in public funds. But then, no authority figure in the Zone cared about its citizens.

Still, Matthias had the right to dock there. The exorbitant fees he paid for the privilege ensured that. Plus, there was the issue of all the best freelance shipping jobs available at the station. But he had a feeling that things were about to get more complicated for him at Antonoff, given that Marielle worked in the dockmaster's office.

"Look," she said. "You've made your delivery here, and

you're free to go. You've been paid. Why don't you take a break from shipping and get your head together?" Her tone brooked no argument.

How exactly could he take a break from shipping, from his livelihood? He, like everyone else he knew, had to work to keep a roof over his head. Matthias wasn't going to debate with her on the breakup front, but he wasn't going to give her ammunition to make his business relationship with Antonoff Station more difficult, either. "I'll be back," he said. "Just don't come out to the hangars when you know my ship's going to be on station."

Without waiting for a response, he turned away and stalked up the access ramp to his ship.

———

Once he returned to the *Ensign*'s cockpit, he checked the freighter message boards for any contracts to pick up that weren't available for pickup or drop-off on Antonoff Station but came up blank. In fact, there wasn't a single contract posted, which was weird.

Maybe Marielle had fucked around with his transmissions. She worked in the station dockmaster's office, giving her access to his some of his ship's systems, and doing so was within her skill set.

He'd try again once he left the station. He requested permission from the dockmaster to depart the station and waited for confirmation, pacing the length of the small cockpit as he did so.

He couldn't believe he'd actually told her he cared about her. It was the most pathetic thing he could have said at that moment when she'd already made up her mind about their lack of a future together. And if, by some chance, she'd reciprocated the words, did he really want to be in a relationship with someone who had to be guilt-tripped into being with him? No, it was best to stay away as best he could, lick his wounds in private, and focus on work. Successful independent freighters could do well in Zone space; it was one of the few professions that could.

His comm board crackled to life, and a voice said, "*Ensign*? This is transit control."

Matthias activated the speaker. "This is the *Ensign*. When can I depart?"

"Your uploaded flight plan doesn't have a destination."

He sighed and tried to keep the irritation from his voice. "I'll upload a proper one once I've cleared the station. I've done that before. I can't access the freighter boards right now."

"Antonoff's SOP states that all departing ships must have a destination included in their flight plans ... "

"Piss off. You've never cared about following SOP before for freighters. We go where the cargo is."

"*Ensign*, I'm going to have to ask you to moderate your language."

Frustration surged through Matthias, and he fought the urge to get out of the ship, go to the transit control office, and tell the bastard keeping him on station what he could do with his standard operating procedures. But that would ensure he would never be able to return to Antonoff Station, not to mention the criminal charges. Instead, he turned to his navigation panel and pulled up his destination file, a list of stations and planets he'd hit up over the last month. One of them was bound to have cheap docking fees and some cargo to haul.

But the list was missing.

God fucking damn it.

His navigation system was working, because he could pinpoint where he was and the immediate area. But his coordinate shortcuts were gone and he didn't have enough time to look them up manually. He launched a search for the nearest guidance beacon on the outer edge of Zone space, just to get away from Antonoff, and honed in on SG-Paradise, whatever that was. It was something small, probably an abandoned spaceport if the scant information posted was accurate.

It was far away from Antonoff Station and Marielle, at least. He could always change his destination once he restored his file.

Matthias inputted the coordinates and uploaded them to the dockmaster's office, and waited.

At last, the voice said, "Thank you, *Ensign*. You've been cleared to depart."

"Finally," muttered Matthias.

"I beg your pardon?"

"Nothing." Matthias severed the connection and activated the freighter's engines. The familiar rumble beneath his boots was reassuring, a perpetual reminder of why he liked living on a ship. He was bound to the Zone's draconian rules and ever-outrageous taxes, but a shipboard life ensured a level of privacy and independence he couldn't maintain living on a planet or station.

The safety lights lining the hangar bay's gigantic doors flashed yellow as it was scanned for life forms, then red as they opened. Matthias plunked down in the captain's seat and strapped himself in. The *Ensign* always gave her occupants a bit of a jolt when she broke dock.

As soon as he cleared Antonoff Station, Matthias tried to pull up his destination file again, then checked the freighter boards for cargo runs using the Zone's public galactic net.

Nothing came up.

"Damn it," he muttered under his breath. Matthias pulled

up his navigation and communication programs, and his irritation coalesced into full-fledged anger.

Someone—and he had a good idea as to who—had wiped out his destination file and disabled his access to the freighter boards. It was fixable, but he needed a place to dock to conduct the repairs and report the hacking, for all the good that would do.

Damn you, Marielle.

It looked like he was going to SG-Paradise after all.

According to his navigation system, the *Ensign* wouldn't be arriving at SG-Paradise until at least midnight on his clock, about four hours from now. Matthias tried in vain to repair his destination file and hone in on something closer, but the extent of the damage to his navigation system meant he had to dock somewhere and start pulling apart equipment. He couldn't very well do that in the space lanes.

He found a bottle of whiskey in the galley cupboard he'd forgotten about when he made his dinner, an obscure brand whose label promised to "pack an extra punch." He eyed it speculatively.

What could one drink hurt?

His communications were largely offline. He'd been dumped by his girlfriend, who he suspected was the one who sabotaged his computers. He was on his way to an obscure outpost in the middle of nowhere that had never shown up on his destination file, any star chart in his possession, or memory until that evening. Matthias deserved a drink.

He uncapped the bottle and sniffed. His stomach recoiled at the odor.

I guess it's technically *whiskey.* It had been taxed as such, according to the big red sticker slapped across the bottle.

Matthias vaguely recalled it being given to him a couple of years back by a client who had some extra bottles lying around.

What the hell. He poured a couple of fingers' worth into a tumbler and tossed it all back in one swallow. It threatened to come right back up, but his throat worked to keep it down.

He stumbled back to the deck-locked table where his dinner waited. *That was more powerful than I thought.*

His last thought, as he fell asleep face-first in his sandwich, was damning Marielle for putting him in this position in the first place.

Something buzzed in the vicinity of his head.

Had Marielle planted an ice wasp nest on his ship, too? Just as a final fuck you?

Matthias raised his head and peeled something off his face. It took a few seconds for it to register as the sandwich he'd made for his dinner, the bread now bearing a distinctive Matthias-shaped indent. He tried to remember how he'd ended up face-planting at his galley table.

The whiskey. My God, what the hell was in that stuff? He'd only had one drink!

The buzzing sounded again, more urgently this time, at least to his throbbing head.

Someone was hailing the *Ensign.* He forced himself to his feet on shaky legs and left the galley for the cockpit. It must be SG-Paradise's transit control.

It was. He turned on the visualizer and speaker, wanting to see who he was dealing with. "Hey," he said, voice barely a croak. "This is Matthias Ericks of the *Ensign.* I'm hoping I could rent some dock..."

The visualizer screen flickered. Great, was that going to go out on him, too?

But the screen's image righted itself, and the smiling face of a stunning woman filled it. Long, silky black hair framed a lovely face with flawless skin, dark eyes, and full lips. Matthias was temporarily struck dumb at the sight.

"You received my SOS!" she said excitedly. "Oh, *Ensign,* thank you so much!" She looked over her shoulder, then turned back to the screen. "I don't know how much time I have," she said. "At least until morning. Do you have a cloaking mechanism on your ship?"

Matthias found his voice, and he cleared his throat. "Cloak... no, this isn't a military vessel. I think there's been a misunderstanding."

She tilted her head to the side. "But didn't you get my messages? I sent them out and your ship acknowledged them."

Matthias checked his transmit log. There were several written messages, transmitted during the hours he was face-first in his dinner, all bearing an unfamiliar origin code.

"I'm here to rent some dock space," Matthias said. "I have some repairs to conduct, and I need to be out of the lanes to do that. Can I transfer some scrip to you, Miss...?"

Her joyful expression immediately shifted to confusion. "You aren't here to save me?"

"What? No, these were the only coordinates my navigation system could pick up. I've never seen them before."

"Because they're for a hidden location beacon," she said. Confusion gave way to devastation, and her lovely eyes became shiny with tears.

Oh, hell. Then another thought struck him. *Save her?* "What do you mean by saving you?" he asked.

"I'm trapped here," she said. "I can't leave. I've been trying to figure out a way to escape, and then your ship showed up and I thought my plan worked." Her voice wobbled, and she closed her eyes for a moment.

"Are you in trouble?"

"Yes," she said. "I need to get out of here as soon as possible. Can you help me?"

There must be a mistake! I programmed them perfectly! I made those distress signals as clear as I could.

Serena fought back a wave of frustration. How many ways were there for someone to say, "I'm being held here against my will and I can't leave without help?" She'd been very clear in her hails to the *Ensign*.

She could be diplomatic with the ship's captain, try to make him see things her way. "How long do you need for your repairs?" she asked.

"I'm sorry?" Confusion carved a furrow into his brow. "I thought you said you were being held on SG-Paradise against your will."

"I am, and if I offer you some dock space, in return, you could help me get off this rock," she said. Her mind worked furiously. If this man could repair a ship, he might be able to help fix her. She hadn't gone into details about what she needed help with on the compound she was confined to in her distress signals, not wanting to scare off possible rescuers, but he needed to know what he was potentially up against if he went through with saving her.

Not if. When. Surely, he had a shred or two of humanity running through him.

"I have some control over my compound's docking bay," she said. She'd managed to hack into that system recently, and Colton hadn't noticed her intrusion. Not yet, anyway. "But I'll need your help actually leaving this place."

He was looking at something off-screen, distraction evident across his features. Serena tried not to notice his strong jawline or dark eyes. It wouldn't do to be distracted herself, even though she so rarely met or even saw attractive men.

He didn't respond to her offer of a docking bay. "My computer tells me you're on a moon," he said.

Serena nodded and tried to keep her patience. "I'm the only person here full-time."

"I don't understand."

It was time to stop being nice. "I'm a prisoner here," she said, her voice sharper and a decibel or two louder.

He finally made eye contact with her again, a gesture that probably would have left her weak in the knees had she been standing.

"I think this area follows under the Zone's military jurisdiction," he said. "I can get in touch with them."

The suggestion sent panic clawing through her. "No! I think the military's part of this!" Why wasn't he getting it? "The guy who's keeping me here has enough contacts with it to get away with what he's doing. I haven't done anything wrong except having the parents I was born to." She leaned a little closer to the visualizer and carefully and deliberately enunciated each word. "I need. Your. *Help*."

His expression was unreadable. "Please," she added softly. "Mister..."

"Ericks," he said. "Matthias Ericks. Just call me Matthias."

"Matthias, please," she said. "If I transmit a docking code to you, can you help me?"

He scrubbed a hand over his face and looked away. Her heart sank. He muttered something that sounded like, "I'm gonna get myself killed."

"I'm sorry?" she said.

"God, what is it with everyone having super hearing today? Yes," he said. "I'll help you, God save me."

CHAPTER 2

THE LOGICAL PART of Matthias's brain told him that he should be more worried than he was about being murdered and his ship hijacked. After all, he was the perfect mark: his ship's communications and navigation systems were down. He'd topped up her factory specs with a few gray market weapons upgrades. When he caught his reflection in one of the viewports, it a man who looked drunker than he actually was, with a small, errant piece of cheese in his mussed hair to boot.

I must have "sucker" written all over me. He flicked away the cheese, not caring where it landed.

But his computers were still capable of telling him that this woman was the only living person in the compound where he was currently docking his ship, and there was something about her that told him she was telling him the truth. Or her version of it, anyway. How the hell she'd ended up on this uninhabitable place, in a compound she likely hadn't constructed herself, was anyone's guess. But as the *Ensign*'s docking clamps connected with the bay's landing struts with a harsh groan, he supposed he was about to get an earful from whoever she was.

He hadn't even asked her name, nor had he recorded their

interaction when she hailed him. God and stars, he was an idiot.

If she planned to kill him, he was handing himself over to her on a platter.

Before he disembarked to meet his hostess in the hangar and ask her about what kind of tools she might have at her disposal, he opened his weapons locker and scanned its meager contents. He slipped a spanner in the top of his boot, something discreet and easily used.

She was waiting in the bay, slim form draped in a heavy black fur wrap of indeterminate animal origin against the chill. Tear tracks marked her face, but she was still smiling. "Hi again," she said. She stuck out her hand from under the folds of her wrap.

He shook it. "I don't think I got your name back there."

"Serena Glazer." Her skin was warm despite the hangar's chill. "The lone resident on SG-Paradise." She looked a little sad at that statement. "So, you're really not here to rescue me?"

"Yeah, about that." Matthias shifted uncomfortably. "I'm a little confused about all this. You *don't* want me to notify the authorities?"

She shook her head, eyes wide.

"So, um—" He thumbed at his ship. "Hop on the *Ensign*. I'll take you to Echo-7. There's a non-military law authority detachment in Center City, and they may be able to help." It was considerably out of his way when he wanted to and pick up some cargo and make money, but if she was in trouble and unable to rely on the Zone military, it was the least he could do.

She looked at the ship, longing clear on her face. "I'd love to, but I can't."

Matthias racked his brain, trying to come up with possible reasons for why a woman being held against her will wouldn't board a ship to take her to safety. All he could come up with was space sickness or some kind of extreme anxiety or phobia. "If you're nervous about space travel, I have a drink that'll take that edge off," he said.

"It's not that. I'm a part of this compound." She held out her hands as if to demonstrate the vastness of herself, but the effect was minimal, considering she was a human.

Or not. Matthias found himself to be a little intrigued despite the situation's gravity.

"I'm an experiment," she said. "My parents were gamblers, they got into debt, and they sold me someone who needed a live body to practice his cybernetics on." Her arms moved under the voluminous black fur, wrapping around herself. "I've been cybernetically modified to fit into this compound. I'm dependent on it. So, as I told you, I can't leave without help."

She spoke the words matter-of-factly, but they had all the impact of a bucket of freezing water being thrown on him. Questions tumbled through his mind, but the one that made it past his lips was, "How does the military work into this?"

"The man who had my parents' gambling debts and took me in lieu of them is in the military."

Matthias had been honorably discharged over four years prior, but he still had friends and contacts in the military and had a working knowledge of the higher-ups. "Who is it?"

Serena's expression shuttered. "Why?"

"I used to be a military man. I might know who it is."

"What?" Her voice bounced off the bay's walls, panic in it. She backed away.

"I was a grunt," he said sharply. "I didn't make it past private. I did the bare minimum when I did my mandatory service." He prayed he wouldn't regret his next words. "You can trust me."

She paused. "Colton Byers."

"Beg your pardon?"

"His name's Colton Byers."

Matthias shook his head. "Never heard of him."

"But he's so important!"

"He isn't," he said. "I served in the Brava System conflicts. All hands on deck and all that. If Colton Byers was someone important in the military, I would've heard of him."

"You just said you did the minimum when you were enlisted."

"Doesn't mean I didn't listen and follow orders. It just means I didn't demonstrate any superior mental or physical abilities." And thank God for that. He never would've gotten out of the service otherwise and made a life for himself on a freighter. Free and relatively easy, away from the bustle, grime, and obscene expenses of the Zone's inner worlds.

Serena was quiet, probably mulling over those pieces of information. "Okay," she finally said. "I can help you with your repairs. In return, I ask that you go back to where you came from and find a way to help me leave this rock. And," she stressed, "We'll have to be quick and discreet about it." She shivered in a way that Matthias could tell had nothing to do with the bay's cold. "Colton will be very upset if he finds out about any of this."

What choice did he have? He had no way of plotting a course back to Antonoff Station without her resources. He could make his repairs, head back, and do some further research to appease her. It was, after all, the least he could do.

"All right," he said. "Let's get started."

Serena tamped down her disappointment at the bitter realization that she would almost certainly not be leaving her compound immediately, but at least Matthias seemed open to helping her.

The *Ensign* was a basic freighter, Falcon-class by her guess. She'd read reports about Falcon-class freighters in her interminable amounts of spare time: they were solid, reliable ships with hardware that could be easily modified with questionable upgrades, necessary for an independent freighter operator to earn a living in a place like the Zone. Her scanners had also picked up a set of laser cannons that weren't quite legal, which were also essential to someone traveling in areas that weren't always patrolled.

She'd perked up when she saw the weapons signatures show up on her scanner. They meant Matthias Ericks didn't always operate strictly within the confines of the law, and that could be helpful in orchestrating her escape.

"So, your navigation and communications systems aren't functioning," she said.

"Nope. Someone fucked around with them back at Antonoff Station," Matthias replied. "I have a pretty good idea as to who." His expression darkened.

"Why would he do that?"

"It was a she, and she did it just to..." He shook his head and trailed off. "Never mind. She did it just to be mean. Probably just to discourage me from going back to there." He steered the conversation back to the matter at hand. "You said you can help?"

"Yeah. Let me get my tool kit."

"I have mine on board."

"My tools are better," she said. "I built my handheld scanner myself." She headed for the bay's door that led to the main compound, then turned around after taking a few steps. "Come on."

He remained rooted to the spot, reluctant. She could read that clearly.

"I'm not going to try anything nefarious," she said.

"Did you just use the word 'nefarious' in normal conversation?"

Some of her excitement leached out of her at that question. "Nefarious" was a great word; it was meant to be spoken. "I did," she said. "I don't get to talk to people that often." She tilted her head to the door. "Follow me."

He did, after hesitating another moment.

While the compound's docking bay was plain and sparse, her actual living quarters were the polar opposite. She noted Matthias's small, surprised gasp as he took in the luxury apartment Colton set up for her: the thick, plush carpet beneath their feet, voice and touch-activated appliances, its tasteful furnishings. Viewports gave her a dismal panorama of the pitted, inhospitable landscape of the moon's surface, an ever-present reminder that she was trapped in a gilded cage.

He glanced out of the nearest viewport. "This doesn't exactly seem like Paradise," he said. "How long have you been here?"

"Around twelve years." She'd last seen her parents, her mother weeping, when she was eleven. She'd hoped they would eventually reclaim her and take her away from this place, but she'd given up on those dreams. It hurt that she'd only stopped fantasizing about them saving her fairly recently. "And 'Paradise' is Colton's name for this place, not mine."

"What?"

His face was frozen in a mask of shock, and Serena had the distinct impression that he only just realized the depth of her situation.

"Twelve years," she repeated. "I've been trapped here for twelve years."

"Oh, my God." He pinched the bridge of his nose between his fingers, grounding himself, she suspected. "Get your stuff. We're leaving."

"And I told you it's more complicated than that." She shucked off her fur stole and tossed it on a couch, then held out her hands. "I'm connected to this place. If I get on your ship and we fly away, I'll die in a matter of hours. I need your help to disconnect and stay alive, and if I'd said that in my distress signals, you wouldn't have stopped."

"No, I would've turned right around for the nearest military installation."

"Yeah, and that would've made things worse."

"Look, Serena, I don't think this Colton guy is as important as you think he is," Matthias said. "I…"

"Maybe not, but he's the one who did all my programming," she said.

"Programming," he said flatly.

"I told you I was experimented on. I even used the word 'cybernetics.'" Had she overestimated her would-be rescuer's intelligence?

Matthias was quiet again. "There was a military cyborg program a few years back," he said, more to himself. "Not much came of it as far as I know, but it wasn't like I was that high in the chain of command."

Serena's breath caught at the mention of cyborgs. "So, you know about us," she said.

"You're a cyborg?"

"Sort of," she replied. "Let me get my kit. I'll help you fix your ship, and I'll tell you what I know in exchange for your information."

"I really don't know that much. Just that the program existed."

"Then it won't take you long to tell me about it." She ran to her bedroom, with its ridiculous canopied princess-style bed that Colton picked out for her, and found her tool kit. It was bulky as hell, but she managed.

"Do you want some help with that?" Matthias asked.

"No, thank you." She was stronger than she looked, was stronger than the average woman, but still weaker than Colton. Her captor had made sure of that.

She picked up her discarded stole and tried to wrap it around herself again, but it kept slipping off her shoulders. "Here," Matthias said and draped it around her and the tool kit. His fingers brushed against her sweater.

This close to him, she could smell his soap and feel his body heat. That sensation was undoubtedly partly the result of her enhancements, but there was something else there, an attraction that reminded her of how magnetic poles always finding one another. It was a strange, thrilling sensation, something she'd never experienced before.

But then, her only contact these last twelve years was Colton. The rational part of her—one of the parts of her brain that he'd enhanced over the years—told her it had to be because he was someone new, and attractive to boot. That she felt that pull because he could be the one who could rescue her and bring her back to civilized space.

But another, smaller part of her, untouched by Colton's meddling, told her something else. She was in the presence of an attractive man for the first time in her life. It was okay, she reasoned, to enjoy that a little. It wasn't as though she could act on those feelings.

His hazel eyes met hers, and she couldn't suppress a shiver running through her at that look, innocent as it was.

Matthias Ericks would definitely be her fantasy fuel for a long time.

He must have noticed a shift in her demeanor because he asked, "Everything okay?" Catching himself, he added, "Besides being trapped here?"

She nodded and tightened her grip on the tool kit's handle. "Yeah. Let's go check out your ship."

Questions and concerns tumbled through Matthias's head, and he had no idea which to ask her first, where to start.

"How are you connected here?" he asked. That seemed as good a place to start as any. As soon as his comms system was back online, he could do some research on this Colton Byers and the abandoned military cyborg program, but those repairs still hadn't been made. He also wanted to talk to Serena; he had a distinct impression that she rarely, if ever, had that opportunity.

Serena slipped off her fur wrap and draped it over the captain's chair in the *Ensign*'s cockpit. She ran her hands over the surface of his comms board in an almost reverent way, reminding Matthias of the times he witnessed baptisms back on Ixon, his home planet. He wasn't sure he heard her and was about to repeat the question when she said, "Colton altered my organs and systems to function alongside the computers in my compound." She tapped at the main comm switch and it immediately lit up. "He used the word 'nanobots' to describe what's keeping me alive and connected."

Matthias had heard the term before but only in the context of the low-budget vids shown in the cheapest theaters on Echo-7. Something inside him clenched painfully at what she was getting at, and a wave of helplessness washed over him in anticipation of her telling him his suppositions were right. "So, you have tiny robots floating through your bloodstream?"

"They're self-replicating and self-repairing microscopic components, but yes," she replied. "They only work when I'm here. If I left, they'd shut down and take the rest of me with them." She brought up his comm's command files with startling ease. "Did you know your comm password was changed earlier today?"

Matthias had to decide which piece of information to

process first: the revelation that she'd asked him to take her away from this place, knowing she'd probably die, or that she could so easily access encrypted files.

She smiled, as if she knew what he was thinking.

"Colton's enhancements made me stronger," she said. "Faster. My short and long-term memory is better than any regular human's. I'm better at fixing computer problems than Colton thinks I am, which is why I was able to get out that SOS." She sighed, and some of the sparkle left her eyes. "I'm supposed to have superior problem-solving skills, but I still haven't figured out the best solution for getting away from here alive." She opened her tool kit and removed a small, flat box, then placed it directly on the comm board. It took a few seconds for Matthias to realize what she'd just done.

"That's a descrambler!" he yelped. "Are you helping yourself to my primaries and passwords?"

"Not helping myself, but helping you."

"You didn't say anything about stealing my personal information!"

"I'm not," she said, tone sharper than he'd heard it before. "You told me you were kicked off Antonoff Station, your comm and navigation systems were down and you could only hone in this moon's coordinates. Someone hacked your systems, and I'm going to help you figure out who did."

"My repairs..."

"Aren't really repairs at all," she finished for him. "Everything done to your ship is easily undone. You can go back to Antonoff Station, beat the hell out of whoever did this, and go back to your life."

"But what about you?" he asked.

Serena leaned against the console. "Will you come back?"

"Of course I will!" he said, more forcefully than he intended. "I'll try to find out more about Colton and your condition, and I'll rescue you as best you can. Did you think I'd just take off and never come back?"

"When you didn't believe me about being held here, and then when I saw how easily your problem can be fixed, I did."

Hurt clawed at Matthias at her matter-of-fact statement. "I believe you," he said. "Do you think Colton's going to do anything to you if I don't take you away immediately?"

"I doubt it." She inputted something on her descrambler. "I just installed an encrypted transmit address so we can stay in touch."

"I'll come back," he said, meaning every word. "I'll look into your parents' whereabouts, too. There has to be someone who knows something."

"I'd appreciate that." She picked up the descrambler. "Your systems are fixed. I'd advise you to change your passwords, though. Someone altered them this afternoon and didn't erase their origination codes if you want to investigate them later."

She abruptly froze in place, head tilted to the side like she'd been hypnotized by an unseen force.

When she didn't move for more than a few heartbeats, Matthias cautiously said, "Serena?"

It was another few seconds before she recovered. "My internal sensors picked up Colton's shuttle's energy signature. He'll be here in a couple of hours," she said. "Damn it! I was hoping he wouldn't return until later in the morning." She shoved the descrambler into her tool kit. "You need to get out of here. I need time to erase your ship's energy signature."

"Are you sure there's no way for you to just come back to the Zone proper with me?"

"Not right now," she said. "But soon. We'll figure out a way." She spoke those words with a confidence Matthias couldn't muster at the moment.

He nodded. "Okay."

She surprised him when she wrapped her arms around him in a hug, and he hesitantly returned it. When was the last time she'd had any kind of physical affection?

"I'll be back," he promised.

"Thank you," she said against his shoulder. "Thank you for not ignoring me."

Tears leaked from Serena's eyes when the *Ensign* departed. She felt a small piece of her heart go with the freighter and hoped like nothing else that Matthias would return.

I've been crying an awful lot lately. It was so unlike her, and if she didn't get a handle on her emotions, Colton would find a way to block them completely.

She'd lied to Matthias when she told him she would be safe here until he came back. Colton had been looking at her differently lately, in a way that made her think he'd stopped seeing her only as an experiment. A wave of pure loathing rushed through her when she thought of the speculative gleam in his eye, the one that always seemed to be present when he spoke to her these days. She would escape this moon or die trying.

She just had to find a way to shut off her nanobots or tweak their programming so they responded to other systems other than her compound's life support.

Serena double-checked to make sure every trace of her SOS and the *Ensign*'s visit was gone, then let herself tune into her surroundings. When she concentrated, she became a part of her compound: seeing everything through the visualizers acting as sentries around the moon and her habitat, feeling the coldness of space around her almost as acutely as if she was outside. She had to remind herself that she could still breathe.

Damn you, Colton. Why are you coming here now?

She had no idea where Colton lived or what he did with his time when he wasn't bothering her on SG-Paradise. She'd been suspecting for a while that he wasn't quite the important figure in the Zone that he made himself out to be, and Matthias, a former soldier, having no idea who he was helped confirm that.

She heard the compound's docking bay yaw open in welcome to Colton's ship, felt the vibrations beneath her feet. She busied herself with watching one of the stupid musicals he'd uploaded to her thincomp, one of the only forms of entertainment he permitted her. She hated musicals.

Colton found her on the couch, her fur stole draped around her. "You're cold?" he asked by way of greeting.

The sight of him had her stomach in knots. Had she been thorough enough in scrubbing all evidence of Matthias's visit from the compound? His voice and body language didn't give anything away.

He was tall, powerfully built, and even with her enhanced strength, she knew she was no match for him in a fight or worse.

He was waiting for an answer. "I just like fur."

He chuckled a little and shucked off his duffel on the carpeted floor. "I thought you would." He inclined his head toward her thincomp. "This again?"

"Why not?" She'd deliberately started the vid close to the end, so he wouldn't have an excuse to sit and watch it with her.

His dark gaze traveled her face, looking for something she couldn't identify. Serena fought the urge to look away. "Is everything okay?" she asked. "I wasn't expecting you for another few hours yet."

Colton blinked. "Yeah. I just felt like checking in." He gracelessly plunked himself into an armchair beside the couch. "How are you feeling?"

Serena parsed her words carefully. "The same."

"Are you sure?"

She hated that phrase. It meant she'd given him the wrong answer to a question he hadn't even asked. She racked her brain, trying to think about changes he could have made to her compound's programming or to her nanobots that he didn't tell her about and wanted her to discover for herself. "I've had more energy lately," she lied. "I'm exercising a little more, reading more."

Her energies were now spent working around Colton's programming and sensors. She dearly hoped she hadn't just given away her activities.

But his only response was, "Huh."

"Yeah." Serena got up, fur still around her. "Do you want some tea or something? I was just going to make myself a cup." She forced a smile to her face. "You didn't happen to bring me some tea, did you? I'm nearly out."

"I brought some." He opened his duffel and removed a box of mint tea cubes. "And I'll have some."

She felt his eyes on her as she walked to the galley nook and set some water to boil. A replicator would have made her life easier, but she suspected Colton hadn't installed one because it gave him more excuses to visit and drop off supplies.

"So, I was thinking," Colton began.

Here it comes. She mentally braced herself as she set out cups.

"Do you think you'd like to leave this place?"

He knows. Her knees buckled, and she nearly dropped her tea cubes. It took a couple of seconds for her to regain enough of her composure to offer a reply. "I can't leave," she said.

"You could if I allowed it," he said. "I was just thinking that you must be getting lonely and maybe it was time to rejoin society."

"Um," she said.

"Is that a no?" There was a dangerous undercurrent to his voice, one she only heard when he thought she was being disobedient or willful. The last time he suspected that he punished her by increasing the compound's heat and gravity controls to nearly-unlivable conditions.

"No," she said. "I mean, it isn't a no. It's more of a surprise. Why do you think I should be out and about now?"

"It's been twelve years," Colton said like she was an idiot.

Didn't she know it. "They've just flown by." The water boiled, she poured it over the cubes in the bottom of the cups.

"I think we should get married," Colton said.

Serena turned around to face him, not bothering to hide her shock. She tried to read his expression, but there was nothing there that gave away anything else he was feeling. He was so still he might as well have been a statue.

She had to clear her throat to find her voice. "What does that have to do with me leaving here?" she finally asked.

"A honeymoon," Colton said. "And maybe introduce you to one of my colleagues. Garrett Jacoby, I told you about him."

"Um," she said again. "Do we really need to get married for me to leave?"

"Think about it," said Colton in lieu of an answer. He crossed the galley floor to where she stood beside the counter, moving closer to her than he ever had before.

The memory of hugging Matthias interrupted the moment and how different it felt to be when she was close to someone who didn't scare her. She remained rooted to the spot, trying not to react when Colton brushed a strand of hair away from her face.

But she couldn't keep her voice from shaking when she said, "I will."

CHAPTER 3

INCOMING TRANSMITS STREAMED across Matthias's comm board as soon as he set a course back to Antonoff Station. He checked his route files: everything was as it should be. The *Ensign*'s systems performed as flawlessly as if they hadn't been tampered with.

It was like watching a religious healing from a Great Faith monk, the way Serena laid her hands on his comm board and fixed everything before he even had a chance to tinker with it.

Serena. My God, she's still trapped there.

He'd been distracted for the few seconds it took for his comm system to respond to the nearest guidance beacon and load his missing mail. As his ship's engines kicked themselves into high gear, he leaned back in the cockpit's captain's chair and tried to figure out what to do next.

Serena had said no military, no authorities. Which left him, an indie freighter captain and former soldier who'd done the bare minimum to fulfill his mandatory military service requirements, as her savior. Matthias was the last person in the Zone, if not the galaxy, who could save someone from a mad scientist if that's who this Colton was. Maybe he should've done more things in the military other than trying to not get shot. He hadn't been entirely successful in that venture, either. The scorch marks left on his left leg and hip from laser fire attested to that.

He'd won a shipping contract he'd bid on before leaving Antonoff Station and his comm array went down, and he sent confirmation that he'd be back at the station in a few hours for pickup. It would be the middle of the night before he returned, or the time most of the Zone designated as night, but hopefully that meant Marielle wouldn't be around to try and kick him off station again. He couldn't believe he'd actually left on her orders, like a dog with his tail between its legs. It was fucking embarrassing.

Remember Serena. You promised to help her.

Right.

He keyed in a search of Serena's name on the public galactic net. All that was returned was a birth announcement, dated twenty-three years' prior, of a daughter born to Grayson Glazer and Faye Pike. Other searches showed Grayson Glazer was, like him, a low-level soldier and Faye Pike, an admin assistant who worked on the never-ending circuit of contract employment on Echo-7. Any other traces of either of them disappeared twelve years ago, around the time Serena said she was interned in the compound.

It looked like Matthias might have to take a trip to Echo-7 at some point in the near future. His heart sank at the thought. Echo-7 was the most densely populated and crime-ridden planet in the Zone's inner worlds, and for the Zone, that was saying something. Just leaving the *Ensign* in the cheapest public dry dock in Center City would set him back hundreds worth of scrip, and he'd still have to make peace with God before offering his prayers in the hopes of keeping his ship from being burgled.

Grayson Glazer and Faye Pike's connection to Echo-7 was

telling. The planet's drug problem was legendary, darfin mostly. Desperate people did desperate things.

Matthias ran another search for Colton Byers, both on the public galactic net and another using his old military ID. There was something more concrete for him to go on with him: forty-six years old, military medic and soldier, and former research assistant for a defunct military-affiliated outfit called Caron Cybernetics. The last part had Matthias's eyebrows climbing.

Unfortunately, that was where the trail ended. There was nothing on his current whereabouts or how he was currently earning a living, at least nothing that Matthias could access.

Damn it.

Frustration churned in his gut at his helplessness. He had no idea what to do next.

Colton spent the rest of the day and night on her couch.

Serena lay frozen in her comically oversized princess bed, stiff with fright and unable to sleep. Colton hadn't spent the night here in years, not since he'd stopped messing around with her body's circuitry to make her sleep and awaken on a set schedule.

She hadn't dreamed during that time. She supposed that was deliberate on Colton's part, but she'd never asked him.

Colton's proposal tumbled through her mind, and she wiped away tears. Of course, he would bring up marriage as soon as she may have found an ally to help her escape. She was fairly certain he hadn't pieced together her visitor from the day before and this was all a coincidence, and when she really thought about it, she should've spotted it coming.

He'd been looking for any excuse to get closer to her over the last year, stopping by the compound more often without any supplies. He hadn't taken any blood from her in months, nor had he subjected her to body scans. In retrospect, he was probably trying to wear her down a little, make himself appear as a viable partner rather than her jailer.

She desperately hoped Matthias meant it when he said he would come back and help her. If Colton hadn't been in the compound, she would have sent him a message already.

Instead, she lay frozen under the pink and purple covers, waiting until a suitable hour to get out of bed without rousing Colton's suspicions.

At half-past five she couldn't take it anymore and got up. She quickly dressed and slipped from her bedroom to the living room-galley, where Colton's still form slumbered on her couch. She suppressed a shudder and as silently as possible set about boiling water for tea.

No such luck. "Morning," said Colton sleepily.

Damn it. "Good morning," she said, trying to keep her voice as bright and chirpy as possible. "Tea or coffee?"

"Whatever you're having."

Serena obediently made tea for both of them. *Please go home. Wherever you live, please go home.*

"Something bothering you?" he asked.

She stiffened. "No," she lied.

"Serena."

There was that tone of voice again. She turned around from the counter to face him. He'd sat up, hair mussed, still wearing yesterday's clothes. She pasted a blank expression on her face and hoped whatever he wanted, it wouldn't be too taxing.

"Yes?"

"I can tell when you're upset about something." He leaned forward a little, elbows on his knees. "It's about what I asked you last night, isn't it?"

What else could she possibly be bothered by? He was the

only human interaction she was supposed to have had. "It was a surprise," she said lightly. She brought the tea over to the living area and sat down on a chair next to the couch, wanting to keep as much space between them as possible. She handed him a cup.

Inspiration struck her. "Maybe we should ask my parents first," she said.

Colton froze, cup halfway to his mouth.

She quickly continued. "Like in the vids you gave me." God, she hated those frothy musicals and fairy tales. But they were pretty much all she was allowed to watch.

He relaxed a little.

"The groom always asks for the daughter's hand in marriage," Serena said. "Plus, I wouldn't mind seeing my parents again."

Assuming they were still alive and wanted to see her. Serena had tried to search for them, but her access to the galactic net was extremely limited.

"You *do* know where my parents are, right?" she asked.

She was treading on dangerous territory now. Colton hadn't tolerated questions about her parents before and she doubted he would now, circumstances be damned.

He took a slow, careful sip of tea, probably formulating a new lie about them.

"I can try," he said. "But you remember that they gave you up, don't you?"

Gave up or coerced or blackmailed, Serena had no idea. She only remembered her mother crying when she was taken away. She seriously doubted that they'd had a choice in the matter.

"I know," she said. "But I thought they'd want to visit with me and you could ask them about the marriage. I haven't had a conventional upbringing," she continued. She steeled herself for what she was going to say next. "I think I'd like a more conventional proposal and marriage."

She nearly gagged on the words, but if Colton picked up on that, he didn't let on.

He stared at her. She remained motionless and stared right back, hoping she hadn't given away her nervousness.

He narrowed his eyes a little, trying to figure out her angle, she guessed.

"You want me to get in touch with your parents," he said. His tone was too flat to read.

"That, and I'd like to see them again," she said. She gave him a sad smile. "Not that I haven't appreciated everything you've done for me these last twelve years, but they're my mother and dad. I'd love to have a chance to get caught up and see how they're doing."

He shifted in his seat, and she realized she'd made him uncomfortable. It was the only bit of power she'd ever exercised over him, and she couldn't say she didn't like it.

She had one more thing to ask. "Are my parents... okay?"

He finally looked away, focusing on the moon's dead landscape outside one of the big viewports. "Colton," Serena said. "Are my parents still alive?"

"They were the last time I spoke to them," he said quietly.

"How long ago was that?"

"*Serena.*"

She heard the warning there but pressed on, keeping her tone as light as she could. "This wasn't supposed to be permanent," she said. "At some point, I was supposed to go back to them, and you've never told me why I can't."

"You're connected to this place," he reminded her as if she could ever forget.

"I know, but they could've visited. Or you could've rewired things so I could leave," she said. "And you said last night you could make it so I could leave and visit your friend with you."

She was pushing him now, but she didn't back down. Matthias was coming back to help her. He'd promised.

She had to believe that he would keep that promise. Her sanity depended on it.

Colton stood up and set his still-warm tea on the coffee table, separating the couch and chair. "I can't speak to you when you're acting like this," he said.

"Acting like what?"

"Hysterical," he said. "Pushy. I'll come back when you can act like an adult."

She nearly reminded him that she was an adult, but knew that doing so would further upset him. Instead, she made her voice as quiet and meek as possible. "I don't think it's unreasonable to want to know more about where I come from, that's all."

Colton shoved his arms into his flight jacket's sleeves. "There's no point in looking back," he said.

Serena knew that was the end of the conversation unless she wanted him to adjust the compound's gravity or heat controls and make her life more difficult. She nodded instead. "All right. When do you think you'll be back?"

Colton paused in front of the door that led to the compound's docking bay. She picked up her fur stole and wrapped it around herself, ready to follow him to the bay's control room like a good captive.

"I'll be back when I get back," he finally said. "I have people to track down for you, don't I?"

Maybe that meant he would hold off on the marriage for now.

Serena nodded.

His mouth quirked up in a smile she knew to be false and

leaned in to kiss her cheek, far too close to her mouth for comfort. She fought back a grimace.

He'd never done that before. It didn't bode well for her.

"I'll see you soon," he said. He inclined his head to the door. "Show me out."

CHAPTER 4

SEALED MUG of strong black coffee in hand, Matthias stalked off the *Ensign*'s ramp to a hangar at Antonoff Station. He'd grabbed a couple of hours of light sleep while the freighter made its way back into Zone space proper, but they'd done nothing to refresh him. Serena's situation wasn't far from his mind.

The station's dockmaster's office was open, staffed by a single clerk who looked as tired as he felt. She blinked when she saw him. "Good morning," she said and yawned. "Sorry about that."

"Don't worry about it." Matthias laid his ident chip on her desk. "Matthias Ericks, *Ensign*. I'm here to pick up a shipment from Elevation Parts."

The clerk scanned his ident chip against her thincomp, then tapped at its screen for a few seconds. "Oh, yeah. It's all ready to be loaded. Is your ship ready?"

"Hangar Four. The cargo bay's open."

"Great." She smothered back another yawn with her hand. "The cargo bots say it'll be a half-hour wait for loading if you want to pick up some breakfast or something."

"I'll wait at the ship, thanks." He didn't trust Marielle to show up and break something else on the *Ensign*.

The clerk looked at him like he was nuts. "But it's so cold in there."

"And I don't want to have to worry about my ex fucking with my ship's systems again."

Her eyes widened. "Did that happen here? Would you like to file a report? I can pass it along to the station authorities."

He considered it for a second. *What the hell.* "Sure. It was Marielle Carver, or someone working for her. She knocked out my comm board and navigation. Have you ever floundered around in space without a reliable navigation system? It sucks."

The clerk diligently typed everything out on her thincomp. "I've alerted the stationmaster."

It seemed Marielle's reach wasn't quite what she thought it should be. The notion was reassuring, though he doubted anything would come from his report. "Thanks." He raised his coffee to her in a mock-toast. "I'll be heading back to the hangar."

"Have a good morning."

The cargo bots were already moving crates into the *Ensign*'s hold when he returned, and there wasn't a trace of Marielle to be found. Just to be safe, Matthias let himself back on to his ship and checked its logs and systems. Everything was exactly as it should be. He breathed a small sigh of relief.

And there was a message from Serena, timestamped just a few minutes ago. He tapped at it.

Her face filled the screen, and for some stupid reason, his heart did a flip-flop.

"Hi, Matthias," she said as if he could reply. "I hope I'm not bothering you, but I'm in a worse situation than I thought. Colton asked me to marry him and spent the night."

Oh, no. The implications of that statement...

But she continued. "Nothing happened, but obviously, my circumstances are a little more terrible for me than I originally thought." She let out a small, nervous laugh. "Um, I'm doing all the research I can into getting out of here, but I can only do so much without Colton figuring out what I'm up to and him punishing me in some way. Please get back to me as soon as you can. He's going to be gone for a while, so I think we have some time." She gave the visualizer a genuine smile. "I hope to hear from you soon."

The message ended. Matthias sank into the captain's chair heavily, his previous exhaustion forgotten.

He hit reply on the comm board and waited.

She immediately answered. "How are you?" he asked by way of greeting.

"Okay," she said. "Pretty shook up for someone who got proposed to, but in one piece. What are you up to?"

"Picking up a cargo run that I'll be dropping off on the way back to your moon, and doing some research into your parents and Colton's backgrounds. You didn't tell me their names, but there was a birth announcement with your name about twenty-three years ago to Grayson and Faye. Do those names ring any bells for you?"

She nodded enthusiastically. "Yeah. Sorry, I was so happy to see you that I forgot to give you that information." She leaned forward. "Are they okay? Colton wouldn't tell me anything."

"Uh, well." No news was sometimes worse than bad news. "They fell off the the galactic net's radar right around the time you said you were taken. I also found out that Colton used to work at a military facility called Caron Cybernetics that was shut down years ago. I've never heard of it."

She tilted her head quizzically. "His work for a cybernetics company I get, but I don't understand everything else. The galactic net covers everything."

"But it doesn't make *sense* of everything, and depending on what part of the Zone you're in, information can be altered or suppressed. Your parents' trail ran cold on Echo-7. It's very easy for someone to disappear there if they don't want to be found."

"Isn't Echo-7 the biggest planet in the Zone?"

"It's the most populated," he said. "It's also the dirtiest, the most expensive, and the darfin problem is really bad there." The illegal drug was the scourge of the Zone, and Echo-7, Center City in particular, was its zenith. "Do you understand what I'm saying about the darfin?" he asked gently.

She nodded but didn't look convinced of his theory. "But my parents weren't drug users."

"That you know of," he said. "You were a kid when you were taken to that moon." Colton Byers finding out about their addiction and exploiting it to get his hands on their daughter for experimentation purposes made sense.

"But there weren't any obituaries?" she pressed.

"None that I found, but not everyone gets a public obit," he said. "They cost a fortune. The galactic net doesn't hold as much information as we're led to believe."

"I just thought what I could access was limited because of the fail-safes I installed to keep Colton from finding out I was using it."

Her knack for bending technology to her will was something Matthias wanted to know more about, but that would have to wait until she could get off that rock. "I'm sorry," he said.

"When you get me out of here, will you take me to Center City to look for them?"

Matthias despised Center City to the point that he refused to do any runs for businesses or people situated there. Fortunately, he'd built up enough of a reputation for his skill in safely navigating the less-savory parts of Zone space and making deliveries on time so he could avoid the metropolis.

But this favor wasn't just for anyone, it was for Serena. "Yeah," he said.

She beamed. "Thank you."

Even through the distance that separated them, Matthias felt her smile on him, bright and warm as the sun.

It was a far cry from Marielle's near-constant state of irritation with him, that was for sure.

He pushed all thoughts of Marielle out of his mind, lest he accidentally summon her and she did something else to fuck up the *Ensign*.

"So, you told me yesterday you're connected to the compound," he said. "I need some more to go on, in layman's terms as much as possible."

She looked away from the visualizer for a moment. "Just a sec, and I can send you the schematics of me and the compound."

Matthias doubted that fell into the 'layman's terms' category he'd asked for, but that was the whole purpose of the galactic net. He could look up anything he didn't understand.

His comm board pinged, and he checked the file. "Thanks," he said. He opened it and waited for it to unpack.

"Basically, my body's systems are connected to the compound," she explained. "Colton created nanobots to respond to my compound and keep me alive. If the compound shuts down or I'm removed from it, my nanobots follow suit, along with my cardiac, brain, and respiratory functions. I've been looking into ways to adjust their function so they'd respond to another environment, but of course, that's difficult to do when my resources are so limited."

She'd told him before that she was bound to the moon compound, but her matter-of-fact recitation of the facts surrounding her imprisonment left him temporarily speechless.

She plowed on ahead. "There has to be a way to completely shut them down and render them inoperable, because I lived without them for the first eleven years of my life, but..."

Matthias found his voice. "What the everloving *fuck*?"

"I'm sorry?"

"He's keeping you as a pet!" Worse than a pet. Matthias had loved his dog.

Serena actually had the temerity to roll her eyes at him. "Well, yeah. That's why I sent out that SOS. I need to get out of here before he reaches his endgame, whatever that is. And I don't think it's marriage."

"That's just another layer to the fuckery cake."

"And it's not like I'd need to be married to be a Zone citizen. The marriage doesn't make sense either."

"Unless it's to cover your tracks," Matthias said. "Force you into a name change and all that, make it harder for you to be found again."

"*If* people are looking for me." She looked a little sad at that thought. Before he could say something reassuring, she said, "You were in the military, right?"

"I'm from Ixon, in the Rims, so I had mandatory military service." Not everyone in the Zone was conscripted: just the working stiffs and poorest of the poor from the Zone's outer Rim Worlds. While Matthias had despised his time in the armed forces, he had to admit that his years of service gave him some economic advantages he wouldn't have had otherwise. Ixon was snow-covered for most of the year, and even though he'd been born there, Matthias didn't think he ever got used to the cold.

"Okay. You said there was a cyborg program. We talked about it."

Matthias remembered. "It was shut down, and I had nothing to do with it. I don't even know how many cyborg success stories came out of it." He remembered the other bit of information he'd dug up about Colton. "I'm sure Caron Cybernetics was behind it."

"But you could find out more," she said. "You're in a better position to find cyborgs than I am."

"There was one that I know of, but he went AWOL years ago." Rather, there were rumors of a cyborg who'd gone rogue shortly after the last Brava System conflict ended, but he knew nothing else about him: not his name nor rank, nor what capacity he served. Given that Matthias had done everything possible to avoid being noticed and get his honorable discharge faster, he hadn't looked into those rumors.

"Will you look for him? There must be at least one out there. What would be the point in hiding me away if I'm the only successful cyborg?"

Before Matthias could answer, his comm board trilled, its chirping noise indicating it was urgent. "One minute," he said. He picked up the comm.

It was the dockmaster's office. "*Ensign*, your cargo is loaded," said the same clerk from earlier. "Bot confirmation just came through."

"Thanks."

"But there's a problem with your account," she said. "We'd appreciate it if you could return to the office and get that sorted before you upload your flight plan."

"Damn it," he said. To the clerk, he added, "Not to you. I'll be there in a few minutes."

"No worries," she said and signed off.

To Serena, he said, "I have to go for a bit."

"Your account?"

"Yeah, and a couple of other things. I'm going to look into that cyborg rumor, okay?"

She nodded, and the light returned to her eyes. Matthias didn't know why, but it was suddenly important to keep it there as much as he could.

———

"God damn it." The epithet escaped his lips before he could stop himself.

Marielle waited outside the dockmaster's office, hand on hip and lips twisted in a petulant frown. "I told you to stay away from Antonoff Station."

"And I told you that you can't just banish me from a publicly accessible station." He brushed past her, the office doors whooshing open with a rusty-sounding creak. The same clerk was behind the desk. To her, he said, "There's something with my account?"

She looked terrified to deliver the news, but he supposed that came with having to be the messenger people loved to shoot at. "Yes. It's been wiped out."

Matthias looked over his shoulder, where Marielle still glowered at him from the doorway. "Did it happen in the last fifteen minutes?"

She nodded. "Yeah."

"Okay. I'm pretty sure Marielle over there has something to do with it." He removed his ident chip from his pocket and laid it on the dented metal desk in front of her. "Can you copy that to restore it?"

Visibly relieved that she wasn't about to be proverbially torn to shreds, the clerk accepted the chip.

Marielle was already stomping away, the sound of her footsteps echoing down the corridor. "Hey!" he shouted. "What the fuck's going on?"

"I don't want you here," she said without turning around.

Matthias quickly caught up with her. "Look, it's one thing

for us to split up, and another for you to try and torch my entire career when I've done nothing to piss you off. What the hell's going on?"

She whirled around. "You took all the good shipping jobs."

He tried to wrap his head around what she was saying. "Yes. That's what I do. You've just described what my job is."

"You take all the *best* ones," she continued. "You took them from my brother and friends. You didn't even give them a chance."

Matthias thought that the utter stupidity of what she was saying might actually short-circuit his brain. "What?"

"You heard me."

"Let me get this straight," he said. "You're pissed off that I have a successful freelancing business with a ship that can handle longer-haul runs to the Rim Worlds—where I'm from —and I have a reputation for making deliveries on time."

She crossed her arms over her chest but didn't respond.

He forged on. "So, in retaliation for this, you break up with me and then wreck some vital pieces of my ship's systems. How in God's name is this logical?"

"You should've given other freelancers a chance to get some good contracts."

"It doesn't work like that," he said. "Does your brother have a ship with the hauling capabilities that mine does? Does he have experience doing those kinds of runs in the areas I go to?"

They both knew the answers to those questions was no. Marielle's younger brother had recently been fired from a long-haul crew and had been looking to start his own freelance business shortly before she split up with Matthias.

"It's not as easy as it looks," Matthias said.

"He won't get experience if he can't get good cargo runs,"

she said. "He can only get those short runs with worthless cargo."

"That's literally what getting experience means," he said. "Doesn't he have a shuttle? You can't do cargo runs with a personal shuttle." Matthias was done arguing with her. The reasons for her actions were so ludicrous he could hardly believe it.

"I'm done," he said. "I've filed a report with the dockmaster's office about your fucking around with my systems, and I'll escalate it if I have to. But leave me and my ship alone."

Without waiting for a response, he turned around and walked away.

CHAPTER 5

COLTON DIDN'T GET in touch with Serena after he departed from the compound, which was unusual: ordinarily, he'd send her messages asking if he wanted him to bring her anything from the Zone, or just wanted to chat with her. He only cut off contact when he was trying to punish her, to make her think he wouldn't return and she'd slowly starve to death or something.

But she didn't mind the lack of contact. If he wanted to punish her, she didn't care anymore. She was very close to finally breaking free of the compound, she could feel it.

Matthias had promised to visit her after he made his latest freight drop, and she nearly vibrated with excitement at the thought of seeing him again. Her heart sped up when she saw him over deep space link: his mop of dark hair and deep brown eyes, the small scar bisecting one of his eyebrows that would have given him a dangerous look had he not had smile lines. He was taller than she was, and Serena knew she wasn't short by any stretch of the imagination, and he looked strong without being intimidating. A nice man.

A nice man whom she already had a crush on. She hoped

she could keep her wits about her when he came back and wouldn't turn into a blithering idiot in his presence.

Plus, he's older than you. She guessed he had eight or ten years on her.

And he isn't cybernetically confined to an uninhabited moon. There was that to consider, too.

When her internal sensors chimed an incoming vessel, she jumped up from her spot on the couch, where she lay sprawled and re-watching the least-insufferable musical in her vid library and grabbed her fur wrap. She was pleased to see that the *Ensign* could still pick up the moon's hidden beacon; she'd made sure his navigation system could recognize unregistered beacons when she repaired it.

Whoever had sabotaged his ship had done her a hell of a favor.

Once she was in the docking bay's control room, she entered the commands to allow the *Ensign* access to the compound and waited.

The sight of the well-worn freighter was the second-best thing she'd ever seen, the first being her captain. Keeping her stole tightly wrapped around her, she ventured into the chilled bay to greet Matthias as soon as its doors closed and it was safe to do so. He looked much better than he had the first time he visited.

"You came back," she said, not trying to hide the excitement in her voice.

"Well, yeah," he said. "Did you think I wouldn't?"

"We've been over all that," she replied. "I keep thinking your showing up is part of a dream, and sooner or later, I'm going to wake up and find out I only have Colton for company again."

His expression immediately darkened at the mention of Colton's name, and she wished she hadn't said anything.

"It's fine," she said before he could ask her about her

captor. "He's gone for now, probably sulking or something." She grabbed his hand, his skin warm despite the bay's cold. "Come on, I did some research. We can compare notes," she said happily.

She noticed as she led him through the hangar to her apartment, that he didn't let go of her hand.

"I didn't find out anything more about Colton that you didn't already know," Matthias said when the apartment door closed behind them. A welcome rush of heat welcomed them, and he let go of her hand to shuck off his flight jacket.

It had been nice, her grabbing his hand.

She didn't seem terribly concerned about his news. "That's okay," she said. "I think I know how we can get me out of here. It'll be risky but worth it."

Something in Matthias quavered in fright at the word "risky."

"I don't think we can remove my nanobots," she said. "But we can reprogram them to respond to another system." She looked at him expectantly, and he realized what she was about to propose.

"The *Ensign*..." he began.

She cut him off. "It has a life support system, right?"

"Of course."

"We can adjust my nanobots to they respond to your ship, in that case."

Matthias stared at her, aghast. "Then you'd be confined to my freighter, and it's not exactly the most comfortable place to be. It's the total opposite of this." He gestured around the luxury apartment.

"You're forgetting the part about it being my prison. The name 'Paradise' is a sick joke."

"I'm not," he insisted. "I'm just warning you that a third-hand live-in freighter is a big change from this. It's darker, colder, the air smells a little funky after being in the space lanes longer than a week or so, and the hot water's limited." He pointed to the vidscreen, where a pair of weepy, wailing actors yodeled at each other about something he didn't care about. "No vids."

"I'm fine with that. I hate musicals."

"You'd be stuck with me, too."

The smile she bestowed on him at that reminder made his heart stutter in his chest, and he had to force himself to keep his expression neutral. Truthfully, saying those words meant it was the first time he'd really thought about that, too.

"I'm sure you're a good roommate," she said. "And I can fix things around your ship. I'll earn my keep."

"What? No, you don't have to do that. I'm here to help you. We're going to get your nanobot issue taken care of," he said. "You'll be able to do a lot more research once you can access the galactic net proper, right?"

She nodded.

"There has to be a doctor or someone who can tweak or remove your nanobots altogether," he continued. "You won't be trapped on my ship forever."

Was it his imagination, or did some of the light in her eyes flicker a little at the mention of that?

"But until then, I can help you do your cargo runs," she said, perking up a little. She looked around the apartment, determination on her face. "Let me get my stuff. I packed a bag already."

"Now?"

She looked at him like he was dense. "Well, yeah. I'm not going to sit around and wait for Colton to come back and rape me or something. I figured something out, and we'll try it. Doesn't the *Ensign* have a sickbay onboard?"

She spoke about Colton and his horrific intentions so matter-of-factly, so calmly, that a wave of nausea crested over Matthias. Once he'd regained his voice, he said, "Yes, there's a sickbay onboard."

"So, we run a diagnostic on me and change the nanobots' programming to correspond to your ship," she said. "I'm not sure if it's a permanent solution, but it'll get me off this rock, at least."

"It seems too easy."

"It is," Serena said. "I mean, assuming it actually works. But you have to remember that Colton did everything he could to hide my existence from the rest of the galaxy. There have to be limitations to the tech he used and I've already managed to exploit some of its weaknesses. The only reason you showed up here in the first place is because your navigation system was wiped and reprogrammed and it could pick up the hidden beacon here. I can be reprogrammed, too."

Matthias was still surprised at that particular feat of Colton's. Creating a beacon and then hiding it from the Zone's massive reach for years was a marvel of engineering. Doing so told him that they were dealing with a very intelligent, very dangerous man, tech limitations be damned.

"If I don't get out of here, I'm going to die," Serena said. "Or worse. I'd rather take my chances with you and the *Ensign*." She looked out the viewport at the dead landscape outside. "It's a risk I'm willing to take."

And it was one Matthias was going to have to be willing to do as well. He could not leave her here in good conscience.

"Okay," he said. "Get your things, and we'll go."

Matthias looked at the small antigrav suitcase, then back at Serena. "That's it?"

She looked down at the sealed case, holding all of her most important possessions. "I don't need much. Do you have laundry machines onboard?"

"Yeah."

"So, you have running water. I have a couple of changes of clothes in there, some toiletries, my tools, and my thincomp. Some towels and a blanket, too. That's it," she said. She surveyed the apartment and all of its useless frills.

"You can bring your things with you," he said.

"All the stuff Colton gave me? All the shit I don't need and didn't ask for?"

"I have towels and bedding onboard."

"Just in case," she said. "I don't want to be too much of an imposition."

"You won't be."

She wasn't going to take any chances of wearing out her welcome sooner than necessary. She and Matthias left the apartment and walked through the docking bay to the *Ensign*'s waiting ramp.

Matthias led her to the freighter's small sickbay, the equipment fairly new. Opening her suitcase, she removed her thincomp and scanner, then checked the ship's diagnostic equipment.

"Are you sure you know what you're doing?" Matthias asked nervously.

No. "Yes," she lied.

She would rather die than deal with whatever Colton had in mind for her. She needed to escape, to find out where her parents were and why they'd left her in his care, to live her life the way she wanted.

Colton constantly harped on how difficult life in the Zone could be for the average person, the high levels of poverty, the lack of economic opportunity. Serena didn't care about that anymore. Forging a life even in a place as inhospitable as the Zone was purported to be better than existing in a gilded cage.

She connected her thincomp to the sickbay computers, uploading all of the information she'd managed to glean about herself and the nanobots. Her plan was simple: changing the nanobots' frequencies to respond to the *Ensign* rather than the SG-Paradise compound's computers.

She activated the program she'd written to do just that, and waited.

Serena thought she could feel the nanobots responding to the new commands, rearranging themselves as they raced through her bloodstream, surging faster through her until they crescendoed into an electric current, so much hotter than she expected. If she didn't know any better, she thought she might be on fire from the inside out.

Dimly, she heard Matthias yelp and reach for her, his terrified expression the last thing she saw as she passed out.

It's still better than staying where I was.

"Fuck!" Matthias's shout bounced off the sickbay's yellow walls as Serena fell back against the diagnostic bed. He sprang into action, opening the med cabinet to find a revival stim. "Fuck, fuck, *fuck*!"

His hand wrapped around a stim tube, but before he could administer it, Serena's eyes opened, and she looked at him, then around the sickbay in wonder.

"It worked," she said. She swung her legs around the side of the bed and stood up, a little unsteady at first.

Matthias set aside the stim tube and reached for her elbow. She wobbled in place for a few seconds before gaining her bearings and checking the diagnostic readout.

"My systems correspond to the *Ensign*'s," she said, unable to hide her excitement. "It really worked!"

With that pronouncement, she threw her arms around Matthias in a fierce hug and quickly kissed his cheek. It was an innocent gesture, but he felt the spot where her lips touched his skin after she broke away, warm as the sun on his home planet during its brief summer.

"You're sure?" he said. "You're *sure* won't die once we blow this pop stand?"

"I am," she said. She wiped away a few errant tears with the back of her hand as she looked at the sickbay's report. "I can't move too far from the ship, but it'll still keep me alive. This could mean the nanobots could be removed or deactivated," she continued.

Matthias had one thing to point out before they left the compound. "We aren't in the space lanes yet," he said.

He hated to see dejection take some of the light out of her eyes, but it needed to be said. She recovered quickly. "Let's go now."

"You're sure?"

She nodded. "As long as I can sit in the cockpit with you."

CHAPTER 6

THE DEPARTURE FROM SG-PARADISE, her prison for so many years, was equal parts terrifying and exhilarating. Serena knew from her diagnostics that she wouldn't keel over once they left the moon; she was now inextricably linked to the *Ensign*, at least until she could get her nanobots removed or deactivated.

And inextricably linked to Matthias as well. While she wasn't happy to still be attached to someone else, he was definitely the lesser of two evils.

You hardly know him, a small voice chided her.

But he was the person who'd responded to her SOS calls, albeit unintentionally. He'd returned to help her escape from the moon. He was going to help her have her nanobots removed.

In a way, she was part of the *Ensign*. Her nanobots could tune into the ship's functions, see her through the visualizers' lenses, feel the whine and groan of her subspace engines. If she wanted to, she could access Matthias's correspondence.

Guilt twanged through her when she thought about how she hadn't told him that part. Maybe he'd already figured it out and she wouldn't have to.

I should tell him. He's saving me from Colton. It's the least I can do.

That, and earning her keep. While lascivious thoughts about Matthias occupied a small, secret part of her mind, there were other, more practical tasks she could do. Laundry, housekeeping, bookkeeping. A freelance freighter operator likely had administrative work to do.

She'd worry about that later. Right now, she would enjoy the rumble of the engines beneath her as the ship broke dock, the thrilling yaw of open space before them as the *Ensign* took off, away from her moon prison.

"How are you doing?" Matthias asked. The freighter dipped a little as it was sucked into space, the groan of the compound's bay doors closing behind it, muffling his voice a little.

"Totally fine." And it was true. Aside from the recycled air tasting and feeling a little different, she was none the worse for wear after having her nanobots' function altered. She would feel it before her heartbeat slowed, or her breathing became labored.

She'd worried a little that she might have a breakdown after they left the moon, some kind of agoraphobic reaction after being trapped there for so long. But now that they were far enough away from it, all she felt was complete and total elation at her escape.

"So where are we going first?" she asked. "What exactly do you transport?"

"Anything that needs to get to Point A to Point B and won't get me in trouble with law enforcement," he replied. "Mostly industrial building materials." He set a course on the navigation panel before him and turned to face her. "I can take a couple of days off. What about your parents?"

Her heart lurched painfully at the mention of them for the first time in years, which surprised her. Maybe it was because she might actually get an opportunity to speak with them and ask what they'd been thinking when they handed her off to Colton. Now that she had that chance...

Matthias was waiting for an answer.

"I don't know," she replied. "Whatever interferes with your life and work the least." The navigation panel pinged, and she saw and felt Antonoff Station's acknowledgment of their flight plan. "We're going to Antonoff?"

"Yeah." Surprise colored his words. "How did you know?"

I may as well tell him. "My nanobots," she said. "They pick up everything."

"Oh." Understanding dawned on Matthias's face. "*Oh.*"

"I'm not going to mess around with your communications or spy on you in your cabin," she said quickly. "I can just pick up transmissions like that."

"You know I ended up at your moon because someone fucked with my computers," he said.

Serena's elation gave way to something dark and ugly, and she felt like crying. She should've told him that was a side effect of the nanobot adjustment. "I'm sorry," she said. "I didn't know it would be this strong." She forced herself to give him a weak smile, which he didn't return. "I couldn't pick up much while I was on the moon, so I had nothing to judge it by."

He regarded her coolly and didn't respond, just turned back to the ship's controls.

Which he didn't need to be at right now since the *Ensign*'s autopilot could safely take over. "Um," Serena said, standing up. "I guess I could do some housework or something."

"I'll take you to your cabin," Matthias said.

She couldn't read his voice like she could the ship's air recycler, and the realization was painful. Her antigrav bag followed them as he stalked off the cockpit and through a dim corridor, its lights flickering. It was nothing serious, she noted, just wear and tear. Keeping the lights bright wasn't a worthwhile expense in the freighter's modest sleeping quarters.

And modest her cabin was. Its sliding door was thin, and when Matthias pushed it aside, she took in the small room, its carpet runner faded but clean, the bed built into the wall in an alcove. Its round viewport revealed stars blurring past as the freighter picked up speed, and a tiny bathroom was installed on the opposite side of the bed.

"There's bedding and towels in the cabinet," Matthias said, pointing to it. "Laundry room and galley are at the very end of the corridor, and most of the equipment works."

She nodded, blinking back tears. "Thank you."

She hated the brusqueness in his voice, hated that she was the cause of it. And hated herself for not telling him about her nanobots' abilities before and letting him make an informed decision about whether or not to rescue her. Her parents might have sold her to Colton Byers, but her own selfishness was going to spoil everything she'd worked for.

He left the cabin without another word, closing the door behind him, and Serena finally let herself cry.

Matthias knew he was being an ass, but he didn't know how to fix it at the moment, and he still had to figure out what to do with the psychic cyborg he'd saved.

Looking back on their interactions, her revelation shouldn't have surprised him. Hell, he should've figured it out on his own. She told him to his face their first meeting that she could sense ships' comings and goings from her compound. She'd lain hands on the *Ensign*'s computers like the monks on Ixon and instantly diagnosed what was wrong with them, then made the repairs like it was nothing. She looked like a woman

—she *was* a woman, he corrected himself—and it was easy to forget she was part machine.

He cringed at the word "machine," recalling the old rumors of the Zone's cyborg program and what he'd discovered about Colton Byers's relationship with Caron Cybernetics.

For the first time, Matthias wished he had fewer scruples and, therefore, more connections to the Zone's seedier sides. Aside from the guy who installed his gray market cannons and modified their energy signatures to keep the military off his back, he didn't have any sketchy people in his life. And Marielle was the person who'd introduced them.

Marielle. There was a whole other headache right there, and he'd plotted a course to go back to the place where she would harass him as much as she could. He could only hope his report to the station's dockmaster would give him results.

And my weapons are gray market. Not totally illegal. The cannons were technically legal weapons he just didn't have a permit for. His estimation of the installer being sketchy shrank a little.

As did his opinion of himself when he thought about how devastated Serena must be right now. The least he could've done was tell her he wasn't angry.

"But that would've been a lie," he mumbled to himself. He leaned back in the captain's chair in the cockpit, feeling a headache coming on. All he could think about at that moment when she told him was Marielle sabotaging the *Ensign.*

He didn't know Serena that well, but he knew she wasn't Marielle.

Damn. He needed to apologize, and now. He stood up.

His comm panel trilled, and he checked the originating transmit address. *Damn again.* He pressed the Accept tab, and his mother's face filled the comm screen.

"Hi, Mom."

"I haven't heard from you in a while," she said. "Is everything okay?"

"Yeah." Through all of the upheavals in his life, he'd forgotten to touch base with his mother. Grace Ericks still lived on his home planet in the Rims, and while Matthias had come to loathe its near-constant chill, he still made an effort to visit when he could. He was all Grace had left of her family. "I've just been swamped with work. How are you doing for groceries?"

The Rim Worlds, while officially part of the Zone, operated as independently as possible, which could make getting imports difficult. Prices were even more inflated there than in the Zone's inner worlds, and the products often inferior quality. Matthias made a point of stocking up on non-perishables and household things in bulk when he could and delivering them to his mother to avoid the Zone's import taxes. He hadn't made a stop there in weeks.

Grace waved her hand dismissively. "I'm fine," she said. "We all are, for the time being. You know me, I'm not shy about telling you what we need and want here."

Matthias relaxed a smidgen and felt less like a terrible son.

"How's Marielle?" she asked brightly.

"We split up," he said. "It was ugly." He didn't feel like rehashing the details.

"Was it you who ended it?"

"Not exactly." Embarrassment washed over him when he remembered asking her for an explanation as to why. "But in retrospect, it was for the best. She threw a couple of the *Ensign*'s systems off to make her point. I still don't know why she did that."

"Huh." Grace didn't seem surprised to hear about Marielle's behavior, but he'd always suspected she hadn't cared for his ex that much. "I'm sorry to hear about that, honey. Did she do any permanent damage?"

"No, but I was lost in space for a little bit." He didn't mention the incident with the whiskey knocking him out. Grace's expression shifted to horrified, and he quickly added, "It was repaired. Everything's running as it should. I'm totally okay, and my heart hasn't been shattered into a million pieces."

"She wasn't the right girl for you," Grace said confidently.

"No shit."

"*Language.*"

"Sorry," he said.

"Matthias?" Serena's voice sounded from the cockpit's doorway. He turned his head to face her.

Her eyes widened when she saw he was talking to someone. "Oh," she said. "I didn't mean to interrupt."

"Who's that?" Grace whispered.

"She can see and hear you," Matthias said.

Serena took a step back in the corridor. "I fixed the galley panel," she said.

He winced. She was trying to apologize for something she didn't have to, for his own crappy behavior. "Thank you," he said. He shifted a little in his seat, to give Serena and Grace a better view of each other. "Serena, this is my mother, Grace Ericks. Mom, Serena Glazer."

Serena looked surprised, but she raised a hand. "Hi."

Grace's image crackled a little over the deep space link, but she nodded. "Hello."

Serena looked a little trapped, unsure of what to do next. "Nice to meet you," she said. She pointed at the corridor. "Um, I'm going to fix the laundry machines."

"What's wrong with the laundry machines?"

"The water washer leaks a little," she said. "And the laser cleanser's a little dull. It just needs a tune-up." She turned away and hurried down the corridor before Matthias could respond.

"Who's Serena, exactly?" Grace asked curiously.

"A friend," he said. "She needs a place to stay for a bit, so she's on board."

"Did she have anything to do with the Marielle situation?"

"What?" Matthias didn't try to hide his outrage. "What the fuck? No, of course not. I'm a lot of things, but a cheater isn't one of them. I met her after Marielle broke up with me, and she's my friend." He hoped he hadn't fucked up that friendship too much.

Grace didn't remind him to watch his language. "All right," she said. "Just asking. Why is she repairing your ship?"

"That's what she does, and I didn't know about the laundry issues." The galley panel being fully functional was a nice surprise.

"You haven't known her long then."

"No, but she was in a tight spot, and I could help." He looked back over his shoulder, at the spot where she'd been standing, looking so forlorn and sad. He hated to see that expression and knew he'd caused it.

Grace could pick up a hint. "I'm going to go," she said. "Come visit me when you can."

"Love you, Mom."

"Love you too, honey. Stay safe in the lanes."

Matthias found Serena in the laundry room, carefully packing up her tools into her kit. "I didn't mean to interrupt your conversation," she said, not meeting his gaze. "I wasn't listening or anything."

"Serena."

She turned big, sad eyes to him, and once again, he was struck by their rich color. *God, she's beautiful.*

But that was beside the point. He tamped down that thought. "I'm not mad," he said. "I don't have any right to be mad, and I'm sorry I put you on the spot like that."

"I should've told you about the nanobots reacting with your ship," she said miserably.

"It was incredibly obvious," he said. "And it's a special ability to have."

"I would like to *not* have that ability," she pointed out. "I just want to be normal."

"Wow, I'm really fucking this up," he said.

"No," she replied. "You're not. And I should've told you. I'm sorry, too."

Matthias could tell that this would easily turn into a debate into who was sorrier, and he wasn't up for that now. Or ever. "Thank you for those repairs," he said. "It'll be nice to not have to boil my own water for coffee anymore now that the galley panel's fixed. And you know you don't have to do any of this stuff. I mean that."

"I want to." She closed her tool kit.

I want to. There was something about the way she said the words that affected him in a way they shouldn't, which reminded him of his inappropriate attraction to her. And he didn't want to be the next Colton Byers in her life.

He willed away his feelings about her, determined to keep them secret forever. "Take a break," he said. "Let's test out the galley panel and see how it boils water."

"Tell me more about yourself." Serena leaned back in the deck-locked chair, sandwich and mug of tea in hand. "I've told you everything about me, and I know almost nothing about you besides what I read about on the galactic net."

Her conversation caught him off-guard. He blew on his mug of steaming black coffee, appreciating the heat and her repair skills. "There isn't much about me that isn't on the galactic net. I was conscripted, served in the Brava System war, was honorably discharged, and returned to civilian life. I got a good deal on the *Ensign*." He rapped his knuckles on the galley table. "And then I registered as an independent freighter operator before the government cranked up the dues and insurance rates to an ungodly amount."

"I thought military service was voluntary in the Zone."

"Not if you're from the Rim Worlds," he said. "The grand plan is to get everyone out of the Rims and into the Zone proper where they can really fleece everyone just for existing. Echo-7 residents pay taxes on the air. It's free in the Rims."

"I had no idea."

"And the air's still dirty on Echo-7." The sheer number expenses associated with living planetside always made Matthias a little more grateful for his decision to live onboard a ship.

"And you think that's where my parents are?"

They'd touched on the topic before, but that was when Serena was still trapped on the moon. Now that she was free, sort of, Matthias would have to gently reiterate what had likely happened to them. "It's the place to start looking," he said. "You said they sold you to Colton for gambling debts, right?"

"Yeah."

"The best place to find someone who could arrange that kind of transaction is on Echo-7," he said. "But it was twelve years ago, and the chances of finding them isn't great."

Her expression shifted a little, but she didn't crumble.

"I just want to know why they did it," she said softly. "I

thought about it, and I'm not sure I want to really reconcile with people who would sell me, I just—I need to know *why*."

"Gambling and darfin, most likely," Matthias said.

She nodded and looked away.

Matthias didn't know what to say, so he looked at the curls of steam rising from his coffee. Boiling hot, just as he liked it.

Serena broke the silence. "You said your ex tampered with the *Ensign* and lives on Antonoff Station. Should I look out for her?"

"You'll be onboard the ship, so you won't have to worry about her."

"I'll keep an eye on your systems," she said. "How long were you together?"

"Just under a year, on and off."

"Did you love her?"

Once again, she'd managed to catch him off-guard. He parsed his words carefully. "I thought I did," he said. It was funny, he'd barely thought about Marielle since he met Serena. Part of that lack of mourning about their split was the distraction of helping Serena, but another part of it was Serena herself. "I think I was ready to settle down, and she seemed okay with settling down, too." He realized the statement was true as he said the words. He'd been settling. "I wasn't expecting her to do what she did," he continued. "It's one thing to break up with someone, it's another to try and destroy their way of life. I still have no idea why she did it."

"What does she do?" Serena asked. "Is she a freighter operator, too?"

"Her family's in the freighter business, but she works for the station," he said. "Administration and paper-pushing, mostly. Why?"

"Maybe she sabotaged the *Ensign* to give her family an edge. Or for her lover. That happened a lot in the vids Colton left for me. They were always so melodramatic."

Matthias had considered that possibility, but it seemed an overreaction to breaking up with him for someone else. "She was pissed that I get good shipping contracts over her brother. If she was cheating, I don't know who it was with." He took a sip of coffee. "Anyway, enough talk about Marielle. It's over, and if that's how she's going to initiate a split, I dodged a huge fucking bomb."

"Is it insensitive for me to point out that if she hadn't wrecked your systems, I'd still be trapped on that moon?"

Her voice was hopeful. Matthias thought he knew Serena well enough by now to know she didn't mean anything malicious by the question.

"No," he said. "Not at all. I'm glad I met you."

CHAPTER 7

THEY MADE a stop at Antonoff Station to pick up some cargo bound for Center City on Echo-7, at Serena's urging. Matthias left her on the *Ensign* with strict instructions to stay aboard, which she planned on doing anyway.

Now that they'd passed checkpoints and beacons into the Zone proper, Serena had the best access to the galactic net she'd ever had. Unencumbered by Colton's technological limits and her own hacks to get around them, she was free to access every piece of information she wanted. She was disappointed to find out that much of the information about the off-and-on war with the Brava System was censored by the government, despite it and the Zone were currently holding at a truce.

Still, she poked around databases, looking for information about her parents and anyone else who could be like her. Logic dictated that there was no way she could be the only enhanced person in the galaxy. She found a few shreds of data that indicated there was at least one other enhanced person out there, a full-fledged cyborg if what she was reading was correct.

She longed to get in touch with Matthias and tell him

what she'd found, but she had no way of doing so at the moment. So instead, she conducted more research.

He'd been screwed over by a lady friend of his, she recalled. A twinge of jealousy flared through her at the idea that he had a girlfriend, but she extinguished it just as quickly. Matthias wasn't hers; in fact, she was pretty sure he had nothing but concerned and friendly feelings for her.

What was her name? Marian?

Marielle. Serena tapped into Antonoff Station's systems and searched for a Marielle, using a couple of spelling variations on her name.

She was easy to find. Marielle was a lifelong station resident, her family having significant ties to the shipping community around Zone space. There were a couple of citations from law enforcement regarding her family's illegal trading with the Brava System during wartime and a few fines for unpaid taxes and undeclared cargo, too. Serena supposed that was the cost of doing business for a big shipping family.

As for Marielle herself... there was an engagement announcement, posted to the galactic net just a day or two ago, for her and a man who wasn't Matthias.

That explained their breakup. Serena wondered how long Marielle had been up to that, and why she had to pour salt in Matthias's proverbial wounds when she damaged the *Ensign.* And it was Marielle who'd done that: Serena could see her digital signatures, her handiwork, all over the engagement announcement and in the hacks she'd made to the freighter's systems.

But Matthias had suspected as much. Would telling him about her engagement do any good? Serena had seen enough melodramatic musicals to know that probably wouldn't be a smart move.

She pushed all thoughts of Marielle and Matthias out of her mind and searched again, this time for someone like her.

And there *had* to be someone like her out there. She keyed in falsified credentials on her thincomp and closed her eyes, concentrating on the device in front of her. With her nanobots, she may as well have been physically connected to the galactic net.

She found snippets of information on a hidden bounty hunter network. Once upon a time, the military lost track of an enhanced soldier and put out a laughably low bounty on him. The soldier's name was redacted in every virtual place she looked, but it appeared that a bounty hunter had taken up the offer. Further digging revealed a name: Janek Dalton, based out of Center City on Echo-7.

Serena smiled. It was a smaller galaxy than she thought.

Matthias managed to successfully avoid Marielle as he arranged his latest cargo pickup. Unfortunately, he'd been informed by three people that she was now engaged, news that made him feel like shit. He'd never been the other man before, and it was a gross feeling. Maybe Marielle had been right and it was time for him to work out of another station for a while.

All he wanted was to stop at Antonoff Station, pick up his perfectly legal cargo, ship it to wherever it needed to go, and return for more pickups without any bullshit drama. Was that too much to ask? He wouldn't even show his face in the station pubs or retail concourses if it meant avoiding getting punched in the face by her fiancé.

And why was everyone so excited to tell him about Marielle's engagement? What kind of fucking sadists lived here?

It was unfortunate that he actually had to avail himself of some of Antonoff Station's amenities while he was here. For one thing, the *Ensign* didn't have a hard goods replicator, and

Serena hadn't brought a lot of things with her when she fled SG-Paradise. She needed clothes, and he headed straight for the nearest retail concourse when he signed out of the dockmaster's office. He also needed to stock up on more food. He was pretty sure she would get sick of sandwiches and replicator-generated soup sooner rather than later.

He ordered flight suits at the first mercantile he came across, sending them to the *Ensign*'s hangar, along with replicator starter, fresh produce, and the most edible non-perishables on the mercantile's product menu. He sent a message to his ship via the comm unit he'd clipped to his collar. "Hey, Serena?"

She quickly answered. "Yes?" Her voice was breathy, like she had been waiting for him to contact her.

"I'm having some stuff sent to the ship. I'll be there in a bit to pick it up. Is there anything you want me to get for you while I'm at the station? I ordered some flight suits for you."

"Oh, fun!" The enthusiasm in her voice over a couple of flight suits made him smile. "Will they have the *Ensign* insignia? Am I an official crew member now?"

"I don't have insignia."

"You need it," she said. "I'll design a patch to sew on our clothes. So I guess if you could get me some thread and needles, I can make patches."

The idea of hand-sewing custom insignia patches for the *Ensign* was one of the most bizarre things he'd ever heard, but if it made her happy, he'd pick her up a sewing kit. "Consider it done." He scrolled through the mercantile's menu screen, looking for something suitable.

I'll be damned, they have sewing and craft kits. He added a couple of each to his order. *Weird hobby, but whatever.*

"I have some exciting news for when you get back," Serena said. "We're going to Echo-7, right?"

Her voice bounding out of his comm unit attracted the

attention of a couple of other shoppers, and Matthias hit the Pay tab and charged the order to his personal account before turning around and leaving the mercantile. "Yeah, but we'll talk shop when I get back to the ship," he said. "We're not on a secure link right now."

"Oh." He heard the understanding in her voice. "I should've picked that up sooner. I can feel that now. Sorry."

"No worries. I'll see you soon." He swiped off the comm with a fingertip.

He walked out of the mercantile, to the crowded concourse. Just before he made it to the hangars, a tall, unfamiliar dark-haired giant of a man blocked his path. His eyebrows were knit together in anger, and Matthias realized with perfect clarity that something bad was about to happen. He hadn't felt that certainty since his stint in the military.

Please don't let me die right now.

"Matthias Ericks?" the man demanded.

There was a question mark in his voice, but Matthias knew whoever the guy was, he already knew who he was. There was no point in denying it. At least the concourse was crowded and people would hear his screams for help. Whether they responded to them or simply started taking bets on who would emerge victorious after the fight, he couldn't say. It was a crapshoot on Antonoff.

"Yeah," he said. The man's gaze latched on to Matthias's, and in that instant, something clicked. "I guess you're Marielle's fiancé."

The guy's only response was raising his fist, aiming square for Matthias, who ducked and ran away, incredibly grateful that the hangar doors opened for him immediately.

"I didn't know!" he yelled over his shoulder. "I had no idea she had a boyfriend until I heard about the engagement!"

He didn't look back, but he heard the man's footsteps

behind him. He was a big guy, but Matthias was faster and outran him fairly easily.

"Congratulations!" he shouted. "I wish you two all the best for a long and faithful marriage!"

The hangar doors cycled open at his entrance, and he prayed they'd close once their sensors picked up his pursuer. They did, and Matthias heard him snarl, "Fuck!" as they shut.

He finally turned around and saw the doors had snagged on the man's flight jacket. But at least he was a safe distance away, and Matthias had managed to escape without a broken nose.

He struggled for a moment, finally tearing his jacket away and giving Matthias the finger through the door's plastiglas window. Matthias made the same gesture back and strode toward the *Ensign*, noting that the ever-efficient mercantile bots were already delivering his order. Cargo bots awaited his orders outside the ship.

He unlocked the *Ensign*'s rampway door, unsurprised to see Serena waiting for him, her fur wrap around her shoulders. His heart gave a funny little squeeze at the sight and the knowledge that she was happy to see him.

Truthfully, he was happy to see her, too.

The freighter's ramp automatically extended. "There's a control panel to your left," he said. "Could you unlock the cargo bay doors?"

She nodded. Before he could tell her that the keypad's numbers and letters were worn away, she pressed her hand against the panel as if in meditation. It was the same gesture she'd made when she repaired his navigation system. She quickly pressed the correct keys, and the cargo bay door lifted with a low groan.

"Should the door make that noise?" Serena asked as she walked down the rampway.

"Yeah, it's nothing to worry about." The words were

automatic, but he remembered again who he was talking to. "Did your sixth sense pick up something I'm not aware of?"

"No," she said. "It's just loud." She wrapped her stole around her shoulders a little more tightly.

"Shouldn't you be on board?"

"I'm close enough to the *Ensign* that I'll be fine," she said. "I could probably go to the station if I wanted to."

"No," Matthias said automatically. "Absolutely not." God only knew what Marielle or her henchmen would do to her.

Or him. He still wasn't entirely sure he'd escaped who he assumed was Marielle's fiancé. It was best to get the cargo loaded and then get the hell away from Antonoff Station.

He directed the waiting cargo bots to load the *Ensign*, then picked up the package the mercantile's bot delivered. He directed it back to the retail concourse. "This is for you," Matthias said, holding the package out to her. "If you need anything else, we can get it in Center City."

He did hope whatever else she needed could wait until they left Echo-7. While he had a decent savings account, just about the last thing he wanted to do was spend it in the most expensive city in the Zone. The only thing cheap about Center City was the rent its sprawling apartment blocks commanded.

Serena opened the package, and her eyes widened in delight at the contents. "I'm a crew member," she said, touching one of the folded flight suits and the sewing kit. "Do you have a preference for our insignia?"

"Well, the ship's named *Ensign*, so something red, I guess." He never thought about it. The freighter's name was emblazoned on her sides in red and white paint, unchanged from the day he bought her. "You really don't have to go to the trouble of making ship patches," he said.

"I want to. Since everything's working on the ship. I need something to do." She tucked the package under her arm and stood beside him, watching the cargo bots.

They beeped in unison and lined up when the last box was loaded into the cargo bay, waiting for further instruction. Matthias ordered them to leave the hangar, and he and Serena secured the ship and returned to the cockpit.

He uploaded a flight plan to the dockmaster's office, praying he wasn't going to be hassled today. "Transit control, this is the *Ensign* requesting permission to depart."

"Acknowledged, *Ensign*." The voice was the same one he'd spoken to the day Marielle fucked up his computers. *The day I met Serena.* He smiled a little at the memory. "We've received your flight plan. Prepare for launch in six minutes."

Matthias ran down his pre-flight checklist and activated the freighter's engines. Serena keenly watched him and would undoubtedly know how to fly a freighter the next time they launched if she didn't already.

The familiar thrum of the *Ensign*'s engines reverberated under their feet, and the hangar doors opened, sucking the freighter into the familiar, comforting blackness of space.

CHAPTER 8

COLTON SMILED a little at the thought of seeing Serena again as he wrapped up his workday's activities at a private lab on Garshan. Everyone who had worked on the military's scrapped cyborg project would be very surprised to see her when he finally showed her off. She'd been his off-the-books mission since before the program was dismantled, satisfying his need to perfect the crude cybernetics the team created when they didn't listen to him with the first one. Serena was proof that he was right about the need for more sophisticated nanobots.

The only person who knew about her was his friend and former colleague at Caron Cybernetics, Garrett Jacoby, who was working on his own projects on a remote planet in the Rims. Jacoby's research aims and successful cyborgs weren't as refined as his, but they were certainly original and had a lot of practical uses.

He couldn't believe he'd actually managed to create something that could interface so easily with technology, without any of the usual cyborg giveaways. Serena looked just like a normal person, without any ports sticking out of her neck or wrists and minimal implants. Plus, Colton had had the foresight to confine her to a compound, minimizing the risk of escape. He was still salty about that fucking cyborg soldier's escape years ago and Caron Cybernetics' subsequent shutdown.

And then the military's top brass, Admiral Best himself, had ordered everyone to halt searching for him. Millions and millions worth of scrip flushed out the airlock because the admiral felt sorry for the cyborg. The fact that the cyborg was his son was immaterial. The bastard should have been more grateful for his enhancements.

Come to think of it, Serena still hadn't thanked Colton.

His good mood caught the attention of one of his colleagues, Fulford. "You have a joke to share with us, Byers?" Fulford asked. They walked down the corridor to the airlock that held personal shuttlecraft, polished boots clanging against the corrugated metal deck. The military's research and development facilities weren't pretty or quiet. He was glad he hadn't raised Serena here.

"No," Colton said. "Just looking forward to taking a load off and a few days' furlough."

"You've earned it. We all have."

Had they? Since the military had ended the cyborg development program, research and development on Garshan had focused on weapons. There were only so many ways they could improve on handheld weapons, and Colton was pretty sure they'd reinvented them a few times since he'd taken to continuing cyborg development on his own terms.

Fulford was waiting for a reply. "I guess so," Colton said.

The airlock doors scanned their bodies for identification, bright blue light flashing in their eyes. The doors cycled open and immediately slammed shut as soon as they walked over its deck tread.

"See you in a few days," Colton said, briskly stalking to his waiting shuttle. It was loaded with supplies and gifts for Serena, with whom he hadn't left on the best of terms the last time he visited her.

"Where the hell do you spend your time, Byers?" Fulford asked. "Every time I've gone to your flat, you're never there."

Colton rarely had reason to visit his quarters on Garshan, spending his time either on his shuttle or visiting Serena. "I get up to all sorts of trouble when I'm not here," he said cryptically.

Fulford barked out a short, humorless laugh as he let himself on to his own shuttlecraft.

Colton had deliberately left Serena alone for longer than he usually did, to let her mull over his ideas and see the mistake she was making in resisting him. It was uncharacteristic of her and incredibly aggravating.

I saved her from her piece-of-shit parents, and this is the thanks I get?

He'd enhanced her in ways neither of them had imagined. He was her only friend, her confidant, and it rankled him that she wasn't warm to the idea of taking their relationship further.

But maybe his leaving her alone for a while had changed that. She would be happy to learn that he could reprogram her nanobots and she could travel with him. He could hardly wait to present her to Garrett, to the research and development team, and then the galaxy, showing everyone in the Zone and beyond that their military was the strongest.

He set the shuttle's course to the compound's hidden coordinates and let the computers take over. It was a ten-hour trip to the moon from Garshan, and he wanted some sleep before he saw Serena again.

Something's wrong.

Colton felt it in his bones when he landed his shuttle in the compound's docking bay. Serena hadn't responded to his hails, and she wasn't waiting for him in the bay's control room the way he liked.

She's dead. I didn't leave enough water or food, and she starved to death ...

But that was silly. She always had a minimum three-month supply of food, water, and air available. Her nanobots could also temporarily adjust her metabolic processes during a calorie shortage.

The compound's lighting, gravity, and air recyclers were working when he stepped into her apartment. The living space was clean, as usual, but there was no trace of Serena.

His panic intensified.

She'd been kidnapped and was now probably dead because of her nanobots. He racked his brain, trying to think of who might possibly know of her existence other than Garrett or her parents, and it wasn't like they knew where she was or even cared in the case of her parents. They'd sold him their daughter with a few crocodile tears for Serena's benefit.

There were no signs of a struggle as he checked the apartment, but he noticed a missing antigrav case from her bedroom closet, along with her toolkit, fur wrap, boots, and a change of clothes. She had only five outfits, all black.

It looked like she'd left willingly.

It was then he spotted the writing on the bedroom mirror, a sticky message written in what looked like the jam he procured from an exclusive shop on Garshan for her breakfasts.

I escaped. Fuck you forever.

He pictured her dipping her fingers in the jar and writing

the damning message, a smirk on her lips. His panic quickly
shifted to rage, coloring his vision, and before he could stop
himself, he planted his fist in the mirror's plastiglas.

CHAPTER 9

EXCITEMENT WELLED up in Serena as she listened to Matthias and a Center City flight controller talk back and forth as he prepared to dock at a public spaceport. She didn't think she would ever stop liking this new life of freedom, the opportunities it presented to her. Even something as simple as creating ship ID patches was the most fun she'd had in years.

A small but distinct voice interrupted her thoughts. *You're still under the control of your nanobots. You still don't know what happened to your parents or why they did what they did.*

Matthias shut off the comm, the staticky noise pulling her out of her head. "Bunch of fucking nutsacks," he grumbled.

"What's wrong?"

"I have to pay atmosphere fees, landing fees, dock fees," he said. "I don't know how anyone lives on this fucking planet willingly." He gently laid his palms on the navigation console, but she had the impression he wanted to slap it out of frustration. "All to drop off some water recycler components." He shot her a quick grin. "But it's worth it."

The last thing Serena wanted was to be a burden. She flashed back to the panic and shame that washed over her when she first boarded the *Ensign*. She knew, no matter how much Matthias assured her otherwise, that he was experiencing all of this extra hassle and expense on her account.

This trip would not be in vain.

Bots took care of the *Ensign*'s cargo unloading; the machines were older and much more decrepit than their counterparts at Antonoff Station. Their unoiled wheels screeched against the hangar's floor, making Serena's teeth ache and she had to return to the cockpit from the rampway to get away from the sound.

From her research, she was able to ascertain the likelihood that Janek Dalton was somewhere in Center City. She didn't want to break into his personal accounts to find his exact whereabouts, thus tipping him off, but she should be able to get a feel for where he frequented easily enough. The last thing she wanted to do was set off a chain reaction of horrible events, which was exactly what hacking would bring her. She couldn't be too far away from the *Ensign*, she didn't want the freighter to be taken into custody with her if she made a mistake, and she wasn't entirely sure that Colton couldn't trace her nanobots.

The nanobots! That was an angle she hadn't considered. *Damn it!*

She'd reprogrammed them. There wasn't a trace of the *Ensign*'s visits to her compound that she could see. Colton would probably only be able to track her if he had the freighter's schematics. She relaxed a little, but the nagging fear that he could be on their tail didn't fully dissipate.

She left the cockpit and returned to the rampway. Matthias was directing the cargo bots. "No!" he said, raising his voice. "Lift!"

The bot's levers remained low to the floor.

"Rise!" Matthias said again. "Upright position! That stuff's breakable!"

The bot's command light remained yellow, indicating that the machine didn't understand the command. Its wheels spun uselessly on the floor.

Serena marched down the rampway to the bot and placed her hand on the top. She could sense where the machine was misprogrammed, and it wasn't something she could fix at the moment. "Its language setting is incorrect," she said. "Standard only functions intermittently. Do you speak Branta?" It was the official language of the Brava System.

Irritation marred Matthias's features. "I picked up a few swear words during the war."

"Do you know any others? Just enough to tell it to take the cargo to the warehouse?"

"Damn it. Fucking Center City." He thought for a few seconds. "*Oufo, deza te tesera.*"

The bot's command light switched from yellow to green, and it took off, squeaking away. Serena couldn't help but feel a little impressed. "Were those all swear words?"

"No, I just ordered it to lift up and go to the warehouse. And that's really the extent of my Branta skills. I can't carry a proper conversation."

The rest of the bots took off with the product, and Matthias sealed the cargo bay. Now was as good a time as any for Serena to tell him about the bounty hunter, see if they could track him down and hopefully the rogue cyborg while they were still on Echo-7.

"I think I found something," she said.

That got Matthias's attention. "It isn't Colton, is it?"

"No, thank goodness. I think I found a bounty hunter who brought in a cyborg last year. He's somewhere in Center City."

His eyes widened in surprise, and he didn't reply. Instead, he stalked back up the rampway and closed the freighter's door. "Matthias?" She hated the pleading note in her voice, and she wondered what part of her statement upset him.

"This is a little out of my pay grade," he finally muttered to himself. "If a bounty hunter is capable of taking down a cyborg ..."

"I could find him," Serena offered. "The bounty hunter, I mean. His name's Janek Dalton. I could get in touch with him and meet him here at the spaceport. I'm sure there's a nearby cafe we could meet at."

"It's not the meeting place I'm worried about," Matthias said. "But I'll see what I can do. I'm just not sure that someone with the ability to take down an enhanced super-soldier won't take the first chance to kick my ass." Before Serena could form a response to that, he said, "If you can find a way to get in touch with him and arrange a meeting, go for it. I'll meet him and see what he's willing to share about that cyborg."

Serena nodded and returned to the cockpit, where her thincomp waited. She had more research to do.

Matthias tried not to think about how much money the spaceport was leaching from him, but when he stopped being irritated about that, he started thinking about Serena.

He'd said goodnight to her over an hour ago, and now he was tossing and turning in his cabin's bunk. He was used to the comforting rumble of the engines beneath him and the silence was unnerving. Almost as unnerving as the probability he'd be meeting up with a fucking bounty hunter capable of taking down a cyborg.

The Janek Dalton fellow Serena told him about had to be a super-human in his own right if he could do that. While Matthias had kept himself in decent shape since his military discharge, he was no match for a warrior. At this point in his life, he doubted he could even shoot a hand weapon with any degree of accuracy.

But he'd promised Serena he'd meet with Dalton. Serena had excitedly told him a few hours ago during a supper of sandwiches and tea that she'd managed to find a transmit address linked to him and sent him a message. Janek Dalton responded and was willing to meet Matthias at the spaceport for a price, of course.

And God and the stars only knew what kind of price he was commanding. Matthias said a silent prayer for his finances and hoped he wasn't being too blasphemous.

He gave up trying to sleep and got out of bed. A quick glance at the chronometer on the wall told him it was half-past two, and he checked Serena's status on the cabin thincomp. Guilt twanged through him as he did so, wanting to respect her privacy, but the life support reading reported she was deeply asleep.

He needed to get off the *Ensign* for a while, needed to clear his head. He dressed and left a note on the intraship system, telling Serena of his whereabouts. It would flash across her cabin thincomp screen once the life support system sensed she was awake.

Matthias left the freighter, sealing the door behind him, and walked through the spaceport. It was busier than he expected given the late hour, although he supposed Center City never slept. It was one of the reasons he detested being there.

It's why I don't want to live on any *planet.* That included his home planet. There was no appeal in living on *terra firma.*

A young, barely-dressed woman touched his arm as he walked past a shop. "Hey, sailor." She gave him a smile that he guessed was supposed to be seductive.

He stopped and looked at the sign above her head. There

weren't any words there, just brightly colored symbols representing different genders. *What the...?*

"You look lonely," the woman purred.

Oh. He'd forgotten that sex work was decriminalized on Echo-7.

"I'm good, thanks," he said and pulled away.

"Well, fuck you, too," the woman snapped at his retreating figure.

Matthias walked past a couple of food kiosks, another selling perfume at outrageous prices even for the Zone, and another brothel, but at least its workers weren't as aggressive as the first one. He found a mostly-unoccupied cafe and moved to turn into it, but he was blocked by a huge, unfamiliar man who filled the doorway.

A frisson of fear zigzagged down his spine, and he immediately began berating himself for walking around a Center City public spaceport in the middle of the night.

"Matthias Ericks?" the giant said quietly.

"Yeah." He remained frozen to the spot, prepared to run if necessary.

"I guess you got my message." He stuck out his hand. "Janek Dalton."

Matthias looked at the proffered hand in shock, then the stranger's face. "Are you serious?"

Dalton looked at him like he was nuts. "Yes. You arrived a hell of a lot faster than I thought you would."

"I didn't receive a message other than the one I got earlier about arranging a meeting. I'm staying at the spaceport and I couldn't sleep."

"Well, whatever, you're here now." He thumbed at the cafe behind him. "Let's get a drink and we can talk about your concerns."

Dalton must have sent a message after he left the *Ensign,*

and Matthias had missed it. *Damn it, I should've checked my messages before I left.* What had Serena gotten him into?

They took seats at a small table near the cafe entrance, where they tabbed in drink orders at the grimy galley panel inset in the tabletop. Matthias stuck to tea, Dalton a double shot of whiskey.

"I see my reputation precedes me," Dalton said when the drinks arrived. "I don't know how you did it, but you found out I tracked down that cyborg a while back."

Matthias nodded, going along with the ruse. "I'm hoping you can tell me where he is now."

"Somewhere in Center City with a woman he met while he was AWOL."

Matthias took a cautious sip of tea. *Ugh.* It was worse than anything his replicator spit out. "Would you have his contact information?"

Dalton looked aghast at the question.

"I have some questions for him," Matthias quickly added. "I was in the military around the same time, I think. I ..."

Dalton's expression remained unchanged. "You think we go out for cocktails and pedicures while we get caught up? Do you even know what a bounty hunter does?"

"A name," Matthias said desperately. "Just his name."

Dalton sucked back half his whiskey in one swallow, with nary a grimace on his face at the taste. "You're fuckin' serious?"

"Yes. And I have some other questions, too," he said. "Have you heard of Colton Byers?"

"What? Are you new to the Zone or just stupid? There are over twenty billion people in this part of the galaxy."

"Matthias!"

Matthias turned around to see Serena, hair mussed from sleep, her fur wrap around her shoulders. He rose to his feet, ignoring Dalton. "What the hell are you doing here?" How far away exactly was the *Ensign* from the spaceport's concourse?

Serena beamed at Dalton and stuck out her hand. "I just got your message," she said. "Nice to meet you."

Dalton looked at her, then back at Matthias. "What's going on here? Who are you?"

"Serena," she said. "I just have some questions about the cyborg you brought in last year."

"The fuck's going on here?" Dalton said. "How do you two even know about that, anyway?"

"I just do," Serena said.

"I just want his name," Matthias said. There was a lot they could do with a name.

"And I'd like to know if you could find my parents," Serena added.

Matthias caught her eye and shook his head a little. She looked at him quizzically, and he remembered again just how innocent she was. She had no idea of what a bounty hunter could be capable of, what kind of connections he could have.

"Not for free," Dalton said.

"How much will the cyborg's name cost?" Matthias asked.

"Two thousand scrip."

God fucking damn it. But the heartbroken look on Serena's face... "You promise you'll give me his name if I give you that money?" Matthias demanded.

Serena gasped.

Dalton held up his hand. "I promise. And finding her parents will set you back forty thousand."

He thought he might have a heart attack when he heard that number. "Can you give us a minute?" Matthias asked Dalton, then turned away without waiting for an answer.

"Serena," he whispered urgently. "I'm sorry. I can't do forty thousand scrip. I don't even have that much in my accounts."

The look on her face tore at him, but she quickly recovered. "I understand," she said. "I'm not mad about it. I get it, I really do."

"I'm sorry," he said again.

"Don't be," she said, voice quivering. "You've already done so much for me. I can't ask for more."

He withdrew his minicomp from his jacket pocket and handed it to Serena. "Do your magic," he murmured. "Transfer the funds. Two thousand scrip."

She turned huge eyes to him. "Are you sure?" she whispered.

He nodded, his heart wrenching both at the look on her face and the expense.

She closed her eyes for a few seconds, concentrating, then tapped at the device before handing it back to Matthias. Dalton removed his own minicomp from one of his trouser pockets and checked the screen. Satisfied at the transaction, he barked, "Lukas Best."

Without waiting for a response from them, he stomped out of the cafe.

"That's something to go on," Serena said, but the excitement in her voice was forced.

"Yeah," said Matthias.

"Matthias, I swear I'll find a way to pay you back," she said. "I didn't know he'd charge two thousand scrip for the cyborg's name."

"I can't believe you arranged a meeting with him," he said, facing her. Fury now rose in him at the incredibly stupid risk she'd just taken. "You don't know what bounty hunters are like."

"Neither do you, that much was obvious," Serena said, her voice rising a little. "How much do *you* deal with them?"

She had him there.

"You should've stayed on board," Matthias said. He

grabbed her hand and walked her out of the café. "You shouldn't be out here. It's too dangerous."

"I'm fine," she snapped. "You know what, it was actually *nice* getting to look around somewhere new."

"Well, we're going back to the ship."

"I feel fine."

But her words were betrayed by a tremble in her voice, and a few meters away from the café, she started to sway on her feet. Alarm threaded itself through Matthias, and he remembered he had no idea how far away she could be from the *Ensign* and still have functioning nanobots.

"Serena?" he said.

"I'm okay," she repeated. But her eyes rolled back in her head, and Matthias barely managed to catch her before she fell.

Oh, hell. He quickly picked her up and, heart beating so hard he thought it might burst from his chest, hurried through the spaceport concourse back to the *Ensign*.

CHAPTER 10

THE DASH back to his freighter felt like it took hours. Matthias was sweating by the time he unlocked the *Ensign*'s door and brought Serena to its sickbay, gently placing her on its diag bed.

How did he revive someone connected to his ship? Shouldn't she be waking up right now? Or was she like a fish who could only be out of the water for a few seconds before suffocating?

Oh, God, not that. She'd come too far to die in a freighter in dry dock at a sketchy spaceport on Echo-7.

He ran a diagnostic on her, including a report on her nanobot function. Her heartbeat was still strong, breathing regular, and according to sickbay computers, she should be awake by now. He wasn't sure how to read the nanobot report. *She has to wake up so she can tell me.*

But she wasn't. Her eyes were still closed in sleep, midnight-black lashes against her cheeks, but at least she looked peaceful.

Coma patients look peaceful, too, you stupid nutsack. So do dead people.

Against his better judgment, Matthias gently shook her shoulder. "Serena."

She didn't stir.

"Damn it, Serena, wake up. You should've woken up by now."

Her head tilted to the side.

"Serena!" he yelled. "Wake up!"

Her eyelids fluttered like she was dreaming. "God damn it," Matthias said, voice cracking.

She opened her eyes and blinked in confusion. He thought his heart might stop. Was this a trick of the nanobots?

"Matthias," she said. "Why are you yelling?"

Relief washed over him, tangible as real water flowing from a shower. He reached for her in a fierce hug, never so glad in his life to see someone wake up.

There was still a question in her eyes when he pulled away a little, but something else, something softer. The look on her face made his heart skip a beat, resurrected thoughts that he shouldn't be having for her.

But she surprised him when her lips brushed his in a hesitant kiss.

He knew he should pull away, but before he could, she kissed him again, more confidently this time, and he was lost.

He kissed her back with a long-forgotten passion, heat roaring through his veins, and everything else that had happened at the spaceport forgotten. All that mattered was Serena and keeping her safe, and how right it felt to hold her.

She broke their kiss and pulled away from him a little. Neither of them spoke.

She pushed herself off the diag bed. "I think I overextended myself," she said. There was a trace of huskiness in her voice that he'd never heard before.

It took a few seconds for her words to register. When

Matthias didn't reply right away, she added, "At the spaceport's café."

"Oh," he finally said. "Yeah. You scared the shit out of me." The disastrous meeting with Janek Dalton and the memory of her collapsing came back, along with his ire that she'd gone behind his back. "What the hell was that?"

"I don't know. That was the first time I kissed anyone."

"Not that."

"Are you mad?"

"About the kiss? No, of course not," he said. "I'm angry that you arranged a meeting with a bounty hunter and didn't say anything."

"You were off the ship when I got that message," she pointed out.

Matthias sighed, a weariness overtaking him. He checked the chronometer on the sickbay's wall: it was a quarter after three in the morning. "Can we just agree that you won't get in touch with bounty hunters without saying something to me first? I don't feel like fighting over this."

"Okay," she said. "At least we have a name for the cyborg soldier. And I promise I'll pay you back for the two thousand scrip."

He'd forgotten about that. Fucking bounty hunters.

"I can do a lot with a name," she added. Then, more to herself, she said, "Lukas Best."

It was totally unfamiliar to Matthias, but it wasn't like the Zone's military was a small one. Except ... "Best," he said, also to himself.

"What?"

"His surname," Matthias said. "There's an Admiral Best in the military. Or there was when I was still enlisted. Maybe they're connected."

Serena nodded.

"But it's not like the name Best is uncommon," Matthias

said. "Maybe they aren't." He looked at the diagnostic panel, needing to bring their conversation back to Serena's wellbeing. "How are you feeling?"

"Fine. Tired, but fine."

"All right," he said. "We've had enough excitement for the night. Let's go back to bed, and we'll talk about this in the morning."

"It's already morning."

"Later in the morning," he said.

She followed him out of the sickbay, and he tried to forget what it was like to kiss her.

Back in her cabin, Serena disregarded Matthias's suggestion of sleep and instead went back to work.

It was true she'd received messages from Dalton in the middle of the night, and when she went to tell Matthias she'd found he'd up and left. Not wanting to squander such an opportunity, she tried to find Dalton herself, hoping and praying that her nanobots would let her keep functioning the further she got from the *Ensign*.

For a few glorious moments at the café, she thought she'd outsmarted them, or at least their hold wasn't as tenacious as she thought. Then she passed out.

At least the stupid nanobots were useful now. She was able to feel the galactic net as she looked for more information on Lukas Best, and she was surprised by what was out there. Much of it was classified or hidden from the public net, but it was still there, and she could find it. She supposed she'd miss that ability once the nanobots were removed from her body, but that was the price to pay for freedom.

She wanted to be normal.

She'd had a taste of that in the sickbay when she kissed

Matthias. A thrill shot through her at the memory, and with it, the need to do it again. He'd been shocked afterward but she knew he'd liked it.

But for now, she needed to make sure that the two thousand scrip he'd paid to Dalton wouldn't be wasted. Ten minutes of illicit searching revealed that Lukas Best's last known address was in a cheap apartment block, a huge structure of tiny, compact units common in Center City, the lease signed with Cressida Merchant.

She had an address, something to go on, and with it, a possible chance at a new life.

And there was something else she hadn't considered before: there was another person out there like her, his body manipulated and adjusted to fit someone else's whims and ego gratification.

My body will be my own again. I'll be able to do whatever I want with it.

Once again, the memory of Matthias kissing her popped into her mind, and with it, a corresponding warmth spread through her. She could hardly wait to do *that* again.

Serena may be inexperienced and a little socially inept, but she could still read his signals, had felt the press of his body against hers. He wanted her, too. Maybe he would be open to talking about that later.

She finally returned to bed, drawing the blankets around her and tried to sleep, if only to make the night go by faster.

Matthias managed to get a few more hours' worth of sleep, but by seven, he gave up and got out of bed. Everything that had happened at the spaceport went through his mind: the disastrous meeting with Janek Dalton. The two-thousand credit payment for Lukas Best's name. Serena passing out at the café.

And then, idiot that he was, kissing Serena when she came to. He still wasn't sure who started that, and it pained him that he might've been the instigator. He cared about her—more than cared about her if he was being honest with himself—but she'd spent much of her life captive. There was a ten-year age difference between them. The latter he could've let go had she not been held on that moon for so long.

He'd really screwed things up, and he still hadn't managed to save her yet.

The object of his thoughts bounded into the galley, where he stared listlessly at a bowl of hot cereal, looking far too perky for someone who nearly died a few hours ago. "Good morning," she said.

She smiled. No, not just perky. Beautiful. "Morning."

She made a cup of tea and sat down across from him at the deck-locked table. "So, this Lukas Best fellow lives in Center City," she said. "He's on the lease for an apartment with a woman. I was thinking we could find them today." She took a tentative sip of hot tea.

Matthias pushed aside the nagging thoughts about how much more it was going to cost him to stay on Echo-7, focusing on her enthusiasm. And why wouldn't she be enthusiastic? She could be truly free, do whatever she wanted. Including leaving him and the *Ensign*.

He wasn't bothered by the idea of her finally living her life for herself, but the thought of never seeing her again made him sad. But until that happened, there were a few practical aspects to consider, ones she would be unfamiliar with.

"If he's living in a unit in one of the big apartment blocks, I won't be able to take the *Ensign* to his home," he said. "There's nowhere in the immediate area to leave her." And even if there was, the dock fees would be astronomical. He'd run some numbers since he woke up this morning, and it might be cheapest to leave the *Ensign* in dry dock here or in another spaceport on the other side of Center City and look for the cyborg on his own.

His heart clenched a little at the thought of leaving Serena, even though he knew she'd be fine on a locked ship. He doubted she'd try to leave again; it was simply too risky.

"There's something else," he said. He hated that he was going to have to bring this up, but the words needed to be said.

Serena paused, her tea halfway to her mouth, perfect lips pursed in a motion to blow off some of the steam rising from the cup.

He felt something twist in him, knowing that what he was going to say would hurt. "What if this guy doesn't want to help you?" he asked quietly.

Except for her eyes widening a little, she didn't react. But he could tell by that small gesture that he'd struck something in her, and that notion hadn't occurred to her before. "Are you prepared to handle that?" he gently pressed. "It's entirely possible that he may not want to have anything to do with us."

Slowly, she set down her cup, then lowered her head. She stared at the tea inside for what felt like an eternity before speaking. "No," she said. Her voice was soft. "I thought... well, I thought he'd be happy to meet another cyborg. *I'm* excited about that."

She tucked a few dark strands of hair behind her ear but didn't look up. "I've been so lonely for years," she said. "I don't expect much from my parents, if they're still out there, but the other cyborg, someone else like me..." She lifted her head, and Matthias saw a fine film of tears shimmering in her eyes. He felt like kicking himself for putting them there.

"I don't want to be alone anymore," she said.

She closed her eyes for a few seconds, and when she

opened them again, she was dry-eyed. But the sad expression on her face was still there, and her hands shook a little when she picked up her tea again.

He was unsure of how to comfort her, but he still tried. "I'm not a cyborg," Matthias said. "I wasn't held on a moon for years or experimented on, at least to my knowledge." He'd undergone countless tests while in the military, and he'd probably been sprayed with something without his informed consent at least once, but he didn't know for sure. "But I'm still your friend."

She perked up a little. "I'm yours, too. But I should tell you I like you more than a friend."

If Matthias had still been drinking coffee, he would have spit it out at that point in surprise. As it was, he stared at her, temporarily shocked into silence. But it wasn't as though he didn't feel the same.

"Say something," she said.

It took him a moment to find his voice. "I wasn't expecting that."

"But we kissed last night," she pointed out. "Well, this morning, if we want to be pedantic."

He still couldn't form a reply to that. Thoughts about their situation—*her* situation, in particular—tumbled through his mind, feelings, and morals warring with each other.

When he didn't say anything, she said, "Is it me?"

"No," he said. "It's not that." It was, but not in the way she thought.

"Is it Marielle?"

"Fuck no," he said. "That's ancient history." He pushed aside his hot cereal, now cold. "It's everything about how we met. Who you are, what you've been through. What you still have ahead of you."

"What if we hadn't met the way we did?" she asked.

"What if I was doing my own thing at Antonoff Station and you saw me at the bar?"

"You'd get my attention," he said. "I think you'd get the attention of everyone into women."

A blush tinted her cheeks, but she continued. "Would you have said hello?"

"If you lived at Antonoff Station, I doubt you'd give me the time of day."

"Yes, I would," she insisted. "Want to know a secret?"

This was an interesting development. He nodded.

"I was so happy when you showed up at the moon," she said. "The first reason being the obvious one, but after that—it was like one of those stupid romance musical vids Colton left for me. A gallant hero saving a princess in a tower."

"I'm not gallant. I had cheese in my hair the first time we spoke."

She gave him a pointed look. "Okay, fine," she said like he'd just missed something obvious. "A hot guy showed up to rescue me. It was a real-life fairy tale, one I never thought would actually come true."

It was gratifying to know she thought that of him. Something in his expression must have given that thought away because the sparkle had returned to her eyes and a smile lifted the corners of her mouth.

He didn't pull away when she closed the short distance between them and kissed him, and this time he let himself enjoy it. He kissed her back, putting everything he could into it, tongue teasing her lips apart, the motion eliciting a gasp from her. Her arms slid around his neck, pulling him closer, and his wrapped around her waist. She trembled against him and could feel his body reacting the same way.

It no longer mattered that he'd rescued her from her moon prison, or that she was still tethered to his ship. At that moment, he was lost in her.

CHAPTER 11

"I THINK I can actually smell the air from in here." Matthias scrunched up his face in disgust as he took in the sight beyond the cockpit's forward viewscreen.

The plastiglas *did* look a little dirtier than it did before they arrived on Echo-7, now that Serena took a closer look at it. Matthias had to hand-fly the *Ensign* through Center City, guided by a disembodied voice from the public spaceport nearest Lukas Best's last known address. He'd cursed a little under his breath as he did so, while Serena pressed her face against a porthole, eager to take in the sights whizzing by the freighter. She hadn't been to Center City since she was handed off to Colton when she was a kid, and she didn't remember the buildings being quite so tall, nor the streets so packed with people. Her parents could be among them.

She moved away from the porthole just as the freighter dipped a little, and she steadied herself. "You might want to strap in," Matthias said absently.

"Yeah." She crossed the short distance to the co-pilot's seat and pulled its safety harness over her chest. She pushed all thoughts of her parents out of her mind to focus on the man next to her, who'd kissed her so well she thought she might combust.

She wanted more of that, but Matthias had broken their last embrace the night before, leaving her feeling strangely bereft. She'd considered following him to his cabin but didn't, not having any idea of how he would receive her.

She didn't need space, but maybe he did. It was just one more thing she had to learn about, one more social skill to acquire. But even she knew it would make things weird if she tried to seduce him.

She could feel a full-body blush overtake her at the very notion. She sneaked a glance at Matthias, whose gaze was still pinned to the forward viewport. "Beg your pardon?" she said.

"The air," he repeated. "It even looks like it stinks. And given what people pay here in taxes, it shouldn't." Some dust and detritus blew at the viewscreen as if to further drive his point home. "My viewscreen plastiglas isn't supposed to be yellow."

Serena peered closer at the viewports, noticing a slight but distinct yellow-greyish tinge to the plastiglas. She didn't remember Center City being so dirty either, but her family had lived in the suburbs, not one of the massive, sprawling apartment blocks Lukas Best was supposed to inhabit.

The comm pinged, a different tone than usual. "Hell of a time for her to call," Matthias grumbled, but there was a small smile on his face as he said the words.

"Who?"

"My mother. And she'll keep trying until I answer." He tapped the Accept tab and Grace Ericks's face filled the lower corner of the forward viewscreen.

"Hi, Mom. I'm in a bit of a tight spot right now." His eyes flicked briefly to his mother's image in the corner.

"Hello to you, too. And what do you mean by that? Did the military re-enlist you?"

"What? No, of course not. I'm just hand-flying this bucket in heavy air through Center City."

"Why are you in Center City?"

Matthias looked at Serena as if searching for an appropriate answer for his mother. "Work," he said. "I had a haul good enough to make the entry taxes worth it."

"Who's with you?" His mother's eyes roved what she could of the cockpit. Serena didn't think she was in her line of vision, but she wasn't sure.

But Matthias didn't try to hide her. "Serena," he said. "You already met her."

Serena leaned over the visualizer in front of Matthias and tried not to let his body heat affect her. Tried, and failed. "Hi," she said.

Matthias's mother smiled, but there was trepidation behind it, and Serena remembered his tribulations with Marielle. His mother probably knew all about that. "Hi," Grace said. "I'm surprised to see you're still aboard. Matthias prefers to work alone."

"Mom!" The *Ensign* dipped again as if to underscore his indignation.

"I'm crew," Serena blurted. "Just helping out for a while." She forced a smile to her face. "Matthias has been very kind to me."

"You hired her?" Grace looked at each of them in turn, fixing her surprised gaze on her son.

Matthias looked away, focusing on something stuck to the viewscreen. Parsing his words, Serena figured. "She's a friend who needed a job," he finally said.

"Marielle ..."

"Marielle has nothing to do with this," Matthias said, voice uncharacteristically sharp. Both Serena and Grace flinched. "And Serena is nothing like Marielle."

Grace's eyebrows raised at that last statement, but she

didn't reply. To Serena, she said, "I apologize. I don't often meet Matthias's friends, and I'm sure you know he's been through a bit of a rough patch lately."

Serena nodded, remembering Matthias's story of being chased through Antonoff Station by Marielle's fiancé. And Marielle's minions sabotaging his navigation systems. But not for the first time, she couldn't be entirely angry at whoever the perpetrator was. The damage brought him to her.

Was it selfish to be glad that had happened?

"We're friends," she reiterated to Grace. "And I'm learning a lot about the freelance shipping business."

Something in Grace's expression softened, and she gave Serena a small nod. "I'm happy to hear that." To Matthias, she said, "I'll let you go. Send a transmit when you can. A visit would be better." She gave him a warm smile.

The sight of it made Serena's heart ache in response, and she fiercely missed her own mother.

"Love you, Mom," Matthias said.

"Love you too, sweetheart." Immediately, Grace corrected herself. "Sorry, not in front of your friends, I know. I love you, Matthias."

"It's fine, Mom."

They signed off, and Matthias shook his head a little. "She still thinks I'm a teenager, too embarrassed to be polite to her in public." The *Ensign* began a sharp descent, and even though she was strapped in, Serena gripped the co-pilot seat's arms for support. "Sorry," he said. "This'll be quick."

"How far are we from Lukas's address?"

"Too far for you to go," he said. "Maybe half a kilometer away from the address you found."

Serena nodded. She'd be stuck onboard the *Ensign*, but hopefully, that wouldn't be for much longer.

Matthias spoke with another flight controller as he navigated the freighter into its dock on an exterior landing pad. His voice rose occasionally as they talked about fees. Evidently, the public spaceport had hidden ones.

Lines bracketed his downturned mouth as he severed the connection with the spaceport controller, but he didn't say anything. Serena mentally added whatever the hidden fees were to the money she already owed him.

He powered down the ship's engines and rose from the pilot's seat. Serena followed suit. "I don't know how long I'll be gone," he said. "I have my minicomp on me and promise me you'll get in touch if anything goes wrong. *Anything*," he emphasized.

"I'll be fine."

"I mean it," he said. "Even if you just want to talk about the decor. But especially if you see or hear anything weird."

"How would I hear anything weird? The *Ensign* is soundproofed."

Matthias gave her a look that said he knew she was being deliberately obtuse, and she smiled. She reached for his stubbled cheek and he leaned into it like he'd been waiting for her to do that.

Something about that gesture made Serena's knees wobbly, innocent as it was. He closed the small space between them and kissed her, sending sparks through her body and making her wish he wasn't leaving the ship.

But he was leaving to find help for her, and she reluctantly pulled away. "I'll see you soon," she said.

He nodded, then lightly claimed her lips once more before he left the ship.

This has to be the most depressing city in the Zone. Even Ixon, Matthias's home planet couldn't compare with the dismal picture before him. His home might be freezing cold and bereft of sunlight for most of the year, but at least its snowy mountains provided beautiful scenery.

Center City, on the other hand, appeared to have taken every effort to obliterate any trees or foliage while more and taller apartment blocks were constructed in their place. They stretched to the perennially gray sky, disappearing into the dirty-looking clouds. Their facades were just as filthy, streaked with decades' worth of grime.

Matthias found the building Serena's research indicated and followed a resident inside. That saved him some time from descrambling its biometric lock. Although, based on the way the other building residents hurried through its corridors and lifts, they wouldn't have cared. There was an air of desperation around the building, a collective aura of hardship and exhaustion. Still, he nodded at a young woman who stepped into the same lift as him and tapped the command pad for her floor. Of course, it didn't have voice commands. Although that worked in his favor since his voice wouldn't be recognized.

The lift shuddered and stalled partway through the trip, and a red error message flashed across the command pad. "Damn it," said the other passenger. She reached for the emergency release bar beside the lift door and pulled it with all her might.

"Want some help?" Matthias asked.

"Sure, thanks."

The bar gave way with a rusty creak, and the lift door opened just enough for them to slip through. Painted on the wall across from them were the words "Eleventh Floor" in the three Zone-recognized Standard dialects, and Matthias tried to look on the bright side. At least he only had to walk up five flights of stairs.

The woman followed him as he ascended the stairs, just as

grimy and rundown as the rest of the building, all the way to the sixteenth floor.

His senses went on high alert. Was he about to be robbed? He had his minicomp in one pocket and descrambler in the other, but no weapons.

Keeping his head down, he hurried to the unit number Serena gave him. The woman paused outside the same door, fear written across her face as she regarded Matthias.

"Oh, shit," she said softly. "I don't remember you, but what do I owe you?"

Matthias stared at her, confused. "Nothing. We've never met."

Some of the tension left her shoulders, but she slipped a hand into her jacket pocket, and he had no doubt she was concealing a weapon there. "What are you doing here?" she asked.

"I'm looking for someone."

That tension returned; he could see it in the set of her shoulders. "Who?"

"Lukas Best."

Now it was her turn to be confused. "Seriously?"

"You know him?"

"He and my sister used to live here," she said.

Matthias recalled that the cyborg's last known address was shared with a woman. "So, you know him," he said.

"Yeah." Her dark eyes regarded him suspiciously, and her shoulders tensed under her oversized coat. "What do you want with Lukas and Cressida?"

"I have some things I need to discuss with Lukas," Matthias replied. "About his time in the military." He dropped his voice a couple of decibels. "About the cyborg thing."

She relaxed again and removed her hand from her pocket. "Are you a cyborg, too? I thought he was the only one."

"No to my being a cyborg." He didn't want to say

anything about Serena. "We just served in the military together."

"Oh. Well, they moved," she said. She looked away briefly. "Partly because of me. Well, *mostly* because of me. It's a little complicated. This is their old unit."

This was getting weirder and weirder. "And you are ..."

"Valenna Merchant," she said and stuck out her hand, the same one that had been in her pocket. Matthias couldn't help but stare at it with suspicion.

"I'm not holding a stunner," she said. "I promise."

He shook it. "Matthias Ericks."

Valenna unlocked the door. "Come on in," she said. "I might be able to help you, and I can give you Cressida and Lukas's new address. It isn't far from here."

He followed her into the flat, and it was just as small and dismal as he expected. "I moved in here a few months ago," Valenna explained. She shucked off her jacket and tossed it haphazardly on a pile of laundry resting on the floor. "I went through some bad, um, stuff and I'm still getting out of it. Cressida and I are almost on good terms for the first time in years." She looked through some clutter on the kitchenette counter, finally coming up with a battered thincomp, its screen a web of cracks.

"So, what should I expect if I show up unexpectedly to a cyborg's apartment?"

"If you're worried about Lukas frying your brains out, don't," Valenna said. "Unless you're there to hurt him or Cressy, of course. But all of the upset between us was caused by me." She looked away for a few seconds before meeting Matthias's gaze. "Darfin," she said quickly. "I'm six months sober."

"Congratulations."

She snorted a little. "Save the accolades if I make it to a

year. I'm only four months out of rehab, and it was my third time there."

"Six months' sobriety is still impressive. I've never used darfin, but I know how hard it is to quit it."

"Well, one day at a time, I guess," Valenna said. "One foot in front of the other, all that shit. This is the longest I've gone without it."

"So, Lukas and your sister gave you this unit?"

"No, there was some time left on the lease when they moved out, and I took it over when I got out of rehab. They wanted a bigger place." She tapped at the thincomp. "I don't know how open they'll be to talking to you," she said. "Especially since I sent you there. But it's worth a shot."

She read out the new address, which Matthias recorded into his minicomp.

"I'll tell them hello for you," he said.

She shook her head. "Don't worry about that. I was surprised that Cressida helped me out with the flat, actually. I really fucked things up last year for them." She pointed at Matthias's minicomp. "Their new place is about a ten-minute walk away. The building's a little nicer than this one." He must have given away something in his expression, because she added, "Nicer for Center City. Believe me, I know what a shithole this whole planet is." Quieter, more to herself, she added, "I need to get out of here if I'm going to stay sober."

Matthias didn't know how to answer that. "Well, thank you for your help."

She shrugged. "You're welcome, I guess. I didn't know Lukas had any friends in the military."

"Brothers in arms and all that," Matthias said quickly. "I just want to see if he's doing okay."

"He is, as far as I know. Madly in love with my sister. It would be cute if it wasn't so gross." She looked at him expectantly, and he knew he was being dismissed.

He moved for the doorway. "Thanks again."

Boredom clawed at Serena, and even though Matthias told her she could contact him for any reason, she resisted doing so.

She ran a diagnostic on herself in the sickbay, downloading all of her information to a memory chip to give to Lukas Best. She let herself into the *Ensign*'s engine room and ran her hands over the machines there, trying to find anything that might need to be tweaked or repaired, and came up lacking. It was the same thing when she checked the water recycler and the laundry room: everything worked.

She went back up to the cockpit and stared outside at the yellow-tinged Center City through the forward viewscreen. The *Ensign* was the only ship docked at the spaceport, and all Serena could see was an endless expanse of the cracked landing pad and soaring apartment blocks.

And a single figure walking toward the freighter, his gait familiar as he approached the *Ensign*. Fear gripped Serena's heart in an icy grip, and she bolted from the cockpit. She was too panicked to check the freighter's specs, see if the plastiglas was two-way.

She ran to the galley, the closest place on the ship that didn't have any viewports, and activated her comm link to Matthias. She hated the catch in her voice as she spoke, hated how she thought she might pass out.

"Colton's in Center City."

CHAPTER 12

MATTHIAS HALTED on the busy sidewalk, Serena's words echoing in his mind. A couple of people bumped into him. "I'll be right there," he said into his minicomp. "Don't move."

"Of course not. I'm not a complete idiot."

Matthias backtracked and made his way through the throngs of people, headed for the spaceport. How the hell was he going to confront Colton Byers without giving away Serena's location? And how the hell had he figured out where she was?

They must have missed something with her nanobots. *Of course, we missed something. Colton Byers* built *her.*

Matthias hated thinking of Serena as being built or enhanced, but she was. She was human with cybernetic modifications. Modifications that Colton could still track, apparently.

His mind raced as quickly as he did, elbowing his way through the throngs crowding the streets. As he approached the spaceport, he pulled out his minicomp and commed its transit office. "I was under the impression there was security at the landing pad," he barked into its speaker. Or tried to. He was a little out of breath from running and panic.

"I'm sorry?" The voice on the other end sounded incredulous. Matthias couldn't blame him. No one would care if his freighter was broken into, but he still had to try his luck with the spaceport's security.

"I was informed by my crew member that there's someone wandering the landing pad," Matthias said. "Given that my ship is the only one there at the moment and this man wasn't wearing a spaceport uniform, I have to assume he's an intruder."

"I—uh, I guess you're Matthias Ericks," the clerk said, stammering a little over his words. He had to be new to the job. Jaded transit officers usually had no problem telling civilians to fuck off. Come to think of it, that was how the entire service industry operated on Echo-7.

"I am," he said. "Captain of the *Ensign* and war veteran. Now, what are you going to do about the security issue on your landing pad?"

"It'll be taken care of, sir," the clerk said.

"I'll be at my ship in a few minutes," Matthias said. "I'd appreciate it if a security escort could meet me at the main entrance."

Curiosity must have got the best of the transit clerk, because he asked, "What exactly do you have onboard your ship?"

The most precious thing he'd ever come across, but Matthias could hardly say that. "None of your goddamned business."

"Understood!"

"About that security escort..."

"He'll be there, sir," the clerk said and severed their connection.

Matthias kept his head down and walked as quickly as he could until he reached the spaceport, where a gray shipsuited man touched his arm at the entrance. "Mr. Ericks?"

"Yeah?"

He pressed a button on the small comm unit strapped to his wrist, and a hologram suspended above it showed Matthias his spaceport ID. "You requested an escort?"

"Yes, and I'd like the area scouted for intruders."

They briskly walked through the spaceport corridors, back outside to the landing pad where the *Ensign* waited, appearing unbreached. There was no sign of anyone, aside from the two of them.

"We reviewed the spaceport's exterior visuals, sir," said the security grunt. "It seems a man did make his way to the landing pad and conducted a quick examination of your ship's exterior but quickly left. We were unable to get an ID on him."

"That's okay," Matthias said. "Thanks for doing that."

"An additional charge for the security check will be added to your bill, sir."

"Of course." Matthias activated the ship's exterior palm lock, then stepped forward for a retinal scan. "That'll be all."

The guard nodded and left.

Matthias let himself on the ship and secured it immediately after. He pressed the nearest intraship key and spoke into it. "Serena? Are you all right?"

It was a heart-stopping few seconds of silence before he heard her running through the *Ensign*'s corridors. Matthias was standing in the airlock entranceway before she launched herself at him, nearly knocking him off his feet, face wet with tears. "It's okay," he said, stroking her hair. "It's really okay."

She sniffled against his jacket. "He found us..."

"Maybe not," he said, but the words weren't as firm as he'd like.

"What the hell do you mean?" She pulled away enough to look at him like he was an idiot. "He knows we're in Center City!"

"And we're going to switch spaceports," Matthias said. "Today. Now. And then we're going to find Lukas and leave."

"You didn't find Lukas?" Her eyes widened in alarm, and something else. Fright. Matthias couldn't blame her.

"His friend's sister is living in that unit," he said. "But she gave me his new address. It isn't too far from here. We'll go to another public spaceport, spend the night there, and find Lukas in the morning. It's too late to be barging into a stranger's home."

"It's only seven o'clock!" she protested.

"And lots of people are sitting down to dinner or changing shifts," he reminded her. "By the time we change spaceports and find his apartment, it'll be dark out. I don't want to leave you at night."

She nodded, mollified. And Matthias realized she still hadn't let him go, nor he of her.

He liked holding her. It felt right.

Serena pressed her mouth to his, and once again, he was lost. A maelstrom of sensations whirled through him, short-circuiting his brain and making him forget all about the dangers of staying at the spaceport.

Both of them were breathing hard when they broke apart, and he reluctantly moved away from her to go to the cockpit and make arrangements to stay somewhere else. "Matthias," Serena said, halting him in his tracks.

"Yeah?"

"Thank you for doing all this," she said.

"We already talked about that…"

"I mean it," she insisted. "Everything I've ever said—about you rescuing me and how happy I was about that, and all your help since I escaped from Colton—it means more to me than you'll ever know."

She paused and bit her lip as if trying to decide what to say next. Matthias waited, but nothing else came forth.

"Let's move," he finally said, and they walked to the cockpit.

It was fully dark by the time the *Ensign* was settled in her new berth, now in an underground dry dock facility with a dizzying array of security features that Matthias was no doubt paying through the nose for. Serena could only hope they wouldn't be in Center City much longer.

They settled in the galley for dinner, sandwiches and soup again. "Who did you speak to at Lukas's apartment?" Serena asked.

"Valerie," Matthias replied, then immediately corrected himself. "No, Valenna. Valenna Merchant. She said she's Cressida Merchant's sister. Just out of rehab." He wrinkled his nose. "She was sort of beating herself up over being sober only six months. That's a hell of a long time to go without darfin." He took a swallow of tea. "I hope she sticks with sobriety."

Serena nodded, unsure of how to answer that. Not for the first time, she wondered if darfin played into her parents' decision to give her to Colton. She couldn't imagine being beholden to a drug that potent.

But would it be comparable to being bound to machines the way she was? Wasn't she as desperate to have her body and life back like someone dependent on darfin? Was it inappropriate to even conflate the two? She didn't know.

Instead, she stood up from the deck-locked table and put her dirty dishes in the galley recycler. She laid her hands on it and concentrated, her nanobots communicating with the machinery within, feeling for any flaws.

"Watching you is like watching a faith healer," Matthias remarked.

"I didn't know those were real things."

"In some parts of the galaxy, like Ixon, where I'm from. There's a significant religious population in the Rims who follow the Great Faith. Not my thing, but whatever floats your boat, I guess." He stood up and put his own dishes in the recycler. "Is there anything amiss?"

"One of your sensors might need to be replaced in the next few months, but that's it. And that's only due to wear and tear." The recycler taking in twice the usual number of dishes was probably the culprit. She removed her hands and, not knowing what else to do with them, shoved them in her trouser pockets.

Well, she *did* know what she wanted to do with them, and they involved Matthias.

Who was standing very close to her, even though he could move away now that his dishes were being taken care of. Indecision warred on his features; even someone as inexperienced and socially awkward as she was could see that. Just as she could see the desire written there, no doubt mixed with uncertainty.

Theirs was an unusual situation.

But while what happened with Colton showing up that afternoon had her on edge, it also reminded her of the frailty of her life. Even though Matthias had pledged to keep her safe and had activated every internal and external alarm available on the *Ensign*, she wasn't naive enough to think that all of her newfound freedom couldn't be snatched away from her on Colton's whim at any moment. Or the military's, for that matter, since that was where the cyborg and nanobot technologies came from. She didn't want to go back to SG-Paradise or be disappeared by the government before she had a chance to live a little.

She curled her hands around Matthias and brought him closer to her. He understood what she wanted, and his head dipped down to kiss her with an urgency that took her by surprise.

It set her senses on fire, every nerve ending and nanobot on alert. His arms slid around her waist, bringing her closer to him so she could feel the hard planes of his chest against her body, his hips pressed against hers. One of his hands slipped under her sweater to rest at the small of her back, searing with a heat that took her breath away.

She slid one of her own hands down his chest, skimming his waist, and experimentally slid under his shirt, fingers stroking his stomach.

"That tickles," he said, but there was a strained note to his voice that she didn't associate with ticklishness.

"Do you want me to stop?" she asked.

He paused for a second, and she thought he was going to say yes. But he surprised her. "Not exactly, but I want what you want. I'm not going to pressure you in any way."

A wave of frustration washed over her. She knew he was thinking about the same thing she was, and she greatly appreciated his sense of honor and responsibility. But she still would've liked to hear him say something sexy or be forward.

It was up to her.

"I want you," she said simply.

He closed his eyes for a moment, and she would have dearly loved to know what he was thinking. "Are you sure?"

"More than anything."

He opened his eyes again, revealing dilated pupils, and a shiver raced through her.

In one smooth movement, Matthias picked her up and carried her from the galley, down the corridors to his cabin. He nudged the door open with his foot and laid her down on his bed on top of the bedcovers.

"Are *you* sure?" Serena asked softly.

"God, yes." He bent over her, knees on either side of her

body, hands bracing themselves on either side of her head. She was surrounded, but not trapped.

And the *look* on his face ... frissons of heat sizzled through her as he regarded her through half-hooded lids. Serena framed his face in his hands, pulled him down to kiss her.

Her hips moved against his involuntarily, the feel of his body against hers intoxicating. He responded in kind in a pale imitation of what he wanted to do to her, what she wanted him to do her.

She slipped her hands under his shirt again, this time letting herself explore his body, roving them over his chest and around his waist to his back. His breath caught in response, and, a little more daring, she slid her hands under his pants' waistband.

He lifted himself off her just enough to pull his shirt over his head, revealing a hard chest that was scored with a couple of old laser weapon-strikes, undoubtedly from his time in the war. He must have caught her staring at them, because he said, "They look worse than they actually were."

She nodded and hoisted herself to a sitting position, then traced a fingertip over the largest one. "Does that hurt?"

"Hell, no." He had a grin on his face as he said the words, but she knew he wasn't laughing at her.

And she was terribly overdressed for the occasion. She reached for her sweater's hem and raised it a few inches, her eyes not leaving Matthias's as she did so. She thought she saw him swallow as she raised it over her head.

A heady sense of power descended over her at the sight. With it, any shyness about exposing herself to him evaporated. He wanted her just as much as she wanted him.

She flung aside her sweater and pulled Matthias back to her, the skin-to-skin sensation better—and warmer—than she could have possibly imagined, a taste of what was yet to come.

He kissed a line down her throat and over the swell of her

breast, strong fingers plucking at her camisole to reveal her nipples, already peaked with anticipation. He took one into his mouth, and Serena yelped.

He immediately raised his head, a questioning expression on his face. Before he could say anything, she said, "It's okay." She smiled. "It's *really* okay."

The last thing she wanted to do was inadvertently convince him to stop doing what he was doing, to freak him out about her lack of experience.

"All right," he murmured, and his head moved back to her breast.

A moan escaped Serena, and she held the back of his head, urging him to keep going. Heat coiled low in her belly, and her breathing had to match Matthias's ragged rhythm. One of his hands pulled at the waistband of her pants, and he lifted his head, another quizzical look on his face. She nodded at his silent question.

She helped him slide her pants off her legs, where they joined her sweater somewhere on the floor, then her underwear. She was now almost totally exposed, and any self-consciousness she might have felt evaporated under Matthias's appreciative look.

He resumed kissing a line down her body, and her breath quickened when he got closer and closer to her center. Her back arched when he finally put his mouth there, drawing a small shriek from her. He raised his head again.

"Don't stop," she urged him. "That was a good sound."

He chuckled a little, then dipped his head to her again.

Serena felt the first waves of climax overtake her, and Matthias her have sensed she was close, felt her legs shaking because he increased his rhythm against her. She came with a shuddering cry, hands tangled in his hair, and still not sated when he moved away and laid next to her on the bed.

"What about you?" Her voice was still breathy.

"Some other time."

Her hands reached for the seal on his flight pants, brushing against his erection as he did so. He looked at it, then her, and nodded his approval.

She unsealed them, and he helped her push them down his hips along with his underwear. She wrapped her hand around him, a little cautious, but when he closed his eyes and groaned, she knew she hadn't hurt him. She stroked a little harder, spurred on by his reaction.

"If you keep that up," he ground out, "This is going to be over soon." Sobering slightly at his own words, he said, "Do you want it to be..."

"No!" Serena said quickly. "I want it all."

That was all the encouragement Matthias needed, and he settled back over her, his knee urging her legs apart. Instinctively, she hooked one of them around his hip, drawing him closer to her.

He urged himself inside her, going slowly, his breath hot in her ear. Serena knew he was holding back, giving her time to get used to it, and while she wanted to tell him not to worry about her, she didn't want to make things any more uncomfortable than they were.

And it wasn't that uncomfortable, really, now that her body could accommodate him. When he was fully seated inside her, she could sort of see what the fuss was about in the illicit books and vid clips she'd pilfered from the galactic net when she could.

But it wasn't until he started moving that she really understood what she'd been missing. It was incredible, this connection to someone she cared about as much as she did.

She could feel the hesitation in Matthias's movements, knew he was forcing himself to be gentle. "I won't break," she murmured in his ear.

"You're sure about that?" She could hear his tension and knew his self-control was at its limit.

"Yes."

He pressed a harsh, possessive kiss to her lips in response and any gentle pretense he had fell away.

And Serena liked it. She could feel another climax building, and she guessed by Matthias's ragged breathing that he was close, too. She bit his shoulder as she came, pleasure coursing through her with the force of an ion storm.

Her name was on Matthias's lips as his orgasm crashed over him, and they lay entwined in the bed for a few moments after, neither of them speaking. She thought she could feel his heartbeat reverberating through him and idly wondered if he felt hers.

"Thank you," she said, settling against his shoulder. She reached for the blankets. "Or am I not supposed to say thank you?"

"I'm not sure. I won't tell the sex council if you won't."

She sat up a little to face him. "That sounds so ridiculous I could see the Zone going either way about that."

"Well, as far as I know, there's no such thing." He pulled her back against him. "Are you okay?" His voice was uncharacteristically shy and unsure.

"Very. If it ever gets better than that, I don't see how anyone ever leaves their bedrooms."

His chuckle warmed her in a way the blanket couldn't. Snuggled against him, she felt herself grow drowsy. Her thoughts wandered as she dozed off, but one, in particular, kept swirling through her mind.

She was falling in love with him.

CHAPTER 13

TUCKING the blanket around Serena a little more closely, Matthias slipped out of bed as quietly as he could. He took a quick shower, and when he peeked into his cabin, he saw she was still sleeping.

Had he lost his mind?

Probably, he mused as he prepared some coffee in the galley. What was more, he didn't even care. Any hesitation he'd held about making his relationship with Serena physical had evaporated, and for the first time in a long while, he felt like all was right with the universe.

Now, he just needed to find Lukas Best and pick his brain. Although now that he thought about it, he shouldn't use those words when he met him. He didn't want Best to think he was trying to break him down and sell his components as scrap.

But when he thought about Lukas, he thought about meeting Valenna Merchant in his place and what a surprise that had been. What if Lukas's trail ran cold again?

"Good morning."

He looked up from his coffee cup to see a sleep-disheveled Serena, who had no business looking as good as she did at this time of day, now wearing her pajamas. "Good morning to you, too."

She crossed the room to the galley panel and set some water to boil, then rummaged the cupboard for her tea cube of the morning. He watched her movements, from her yawn to taking her first sip of tea. She settled in at the table next to him. "How are you?" she asked.

"I should be asking you that question. And I'm fine," he said. "You?"

She gave him a coy, sexy smile. "Better than fine."

He leaned in to kiss her, and she melted into him. He had to remind himself what he needed to do that morning before either of them got carried away, and he reluctantly broke their contact.

As if she could read his mind, she said, "I wish I could go with you today."

"I'll see if Lukas could come here."

She stood up suddenly. "I forgot to give you something last night, to take to Lukas. Let me get it."

"It isn't like you to forget something."

"You distracted me." She bolted from the galley—also with more energy than he would have expected given the time of day—calling over her shoulder, "It's in my cabin!"

She returned a minute later and held out her hand. In her palm lay a memory chip.

Matthias picked it up. "What's this for?"

"It's my schematics," she said. "Everything I know about my nanobots, everything I know about Colton. I did a full diagnostic on myself while you were out yesterday and downloaded everything from the sickbay computers on to it. If Lukas is anything like me, personality-wise, he'll want to see it." She closed his hand over the chip like she was giving him something precious.

And she was. Everything about her was on it.

Everything that made her cybernetic, he corrected himself. She'd spoken about personalities, but that wouldn't be on the chip.

"It should work with any hardware," Serena said. "It isn't encrypted either, for ease of use, so don't lose it."

"I'll guard it with my life." He tried to inject a little levity into his voice and failed. They *were* talking about her life, after all.

But she still managed a smile. "I know you will."

The *Ensign* secured with Serena onboard, Matthias left the ship and started walking briskly in the direction of Lukas Best's new apartment. He hoped nine o'clock wasn't too early in the morning to come calling; he hadn't had to make an unannounced social visit in years.

When was the last time he'd had to do that? He racked his brain and came up with the time when he was ten or eleven and his mother ordered him to the neighbors to ask for a bag of sweetener. Being Ixon, a planet in the Rims meant supplies were often scarce. Matthias had ended up trading four scrip and a bottle of vegetable oil for the sweetener, and it only ended up being half a bag, anyway.

What if he was at work? Did former military cyborg just up and get normal jobs? He had no idea.

Center City's streets weren't quite as crowded at this time of the day, and Matthias thought the yellow-gray haze of pollution might be a little lighter in color, too. The smell of coffee from a street vendor—real coffee, not the shitty replicated stuff his galley provided—was tempting, but he moved on. He couldn't be sure that it wasn't adulterated with something, nor did he want to waste any time getting to Lukas's apartment.

The building Valenna told him to go to was a little nicer than the one he'd been to the day before, but that was where the similarities ended. It was just as blocky and ugly as the other one, grimy plastiglas windows tinted dark, the structure reaching high into the sky. Staring up at it, Matthias thought it might actually sway in high winds, and he suppressed an involuntary shudder.

There was nothing better than living on a ship. He would never sacrifice his freedom for living planetside.

But would Serena feel the same way?

His heart ached at the thought of her leaving the *Ensign*, but that was the whole point of his being here: to secure her freedom. Including the choice to leave him if she wanted to, and finally, experience truly *living*.

He brushed aside any thought of Serena and what they'd shared the night before, not wanting to distract himself.

Matthias followed someone inside the flat block, a little incredulous that on a planet known for its obscene crime rates that no one seemed to care about security. At least the lifts worked in this building, he noted. He strode along the twenty-first floor's corridor until he came to the unit Valenna told him about.

He knocked on the door and held his breath, waiting.

An intercom crackled. "Who is it?" The voice was feminine.

Someone was home! Hopefully, she would be willing to speak with him. "My name's Matthias Ericks," he said. "I'm looking for Lukas Best."

He waited for a reply, but none came.

If not for the intercom static, Matthias would have thought he'd been dismissed. "Please," he said. "I'm not here to cause trouble. I know someone in the same situation he's been in, and she needs his help."

"What did you say your name is again?" she asked.

"Matthias Ericks. I was in the military, but I never served with him."

There was another pause, and the door opened.

A slender woman with long, dark hair tied in a ponytail stood in the doorway. She bore a remarkable resemblance to Valenna, but seemed less... twitchy, Matthias thought. She didn't have the same haunted look Valenna had. "Hi," he said.

From behind her, a taller man loomed. A port in the side of his neck was barely concealed by his sweater's collar. "Yes?" he said.

"You're Lukas Best?"

He nodded.

Now that he'd finally found the rogue cyborg, Matthias didn't know where to start. "May I come in?" he asked. "If I'm not interrupting anything."

"Our breakfast is over, so no." Matthias heard the suspicion in Lukas's voice.

Valenna's sister looked at Lukas, and they exchanged a look, the kind only couples had.

She opened the door enough for Matthias to step into the flat. "Come on in," she said. "How did you find us?"

"Valenna Merchant."

Lukas's eyes narrowed at the mention of her name, and the woman's nostrils flared. "I see. Well, I'm Cressida, her sister." She sighed. "I'm sorry, I don't mean to take out my frustration on you. I would've preferred if she contacted us before giving a stranger our address."

"Valenna mentioned that you're, uh, not on the best of terms." Matthias stuffed his hands in his pockets and looked around the apartment. It was nicer than Valenna's, with a real bedroom off the living area. It was neat as a pin, the walls decorated with holos.

"That's the kindest thing Valenna's ever said," Lukas

muttered. He went to the kitchen nook and shoved a couple of plates into the wall-mounted recycler.

Cressida shot him another look but didn't comment on that. "We have a complicated relationship with her," she explained.

"She mentioned she got out of rehab recently."

"Yeah. I cut her off a while ago and that was the push for her to get her life together," Cressida said. She motioned to a chair. "Please sit down."

Matthias did as he was told. Cressida sat down on a small couch across from him, and Lukas joined her.

"You said you know someone who's in the same position as I was," Lukas said. "Cyborg?"

Matthias nodded. "Yeah, but an advanced cyborg."

Lukas stared at him like he was an idiot.

"Her name's Serena Glazer. She's been programmed with nanobots." He cringed. "I really hate the word 'programmed.'"

"Don't worry about it," Lukas said. "Although I hate it, too." He rested his elbows on his knees and leaned in a little closer. "You're telling me you know a female cyborg who's been enhanced just with nanobots?"

Matthias's heart sank a little. "You don't know about her?"

"No. As far as I know, I'm the only cyborg the military and Caron Cybernetics ever successfully produced. *But*," he stressed, "The Zone and its military are full of shady characters. I wouldn't be surprised if there are more."

"She was confined to a moon with a hidden location beacon for the last twelve years," Matthias said. "I found her by accident. Her nanobots were programmed to keep her internal life support connected to the moon compound. She reprogrammed herself to respond to my ship instead, but she's still trapped on it. It's a different kind of prison."

Now both of them stared at him, aghast.

What if they couldn't help her? He hadn't let himself imagine that scenario. It was too awful to contemplate.

"Does she have any ports?" Cressida finally asked.

To illustrate her point, Lukas rolled up his sweater's sleeve, revealing one in his wrist.

"No, nothing like that." If he hadn't known that before last night, he would know it now, but it wasn't like he was about to explain that to Lukas and Cressida. "But she can communicate, I guess, with machines. It's like watching one of those Great Faith monks, only she can actually diagnose and repair issues with the laying of hands." He thought about her other cyborg capabilities. "She's very strong and can solve problems instantly. She says her enhancements are exceptional, but I don't have much to go on to compare it to."

"All right," Lukas said. "What else? How did she end up on that moon?"

Matthias began by telling them about how his ship's navigation system was sabotaged and he ended up at Serena's moon accidentally, about answering her distress call and learning about her being sold and her confinement. As he continued his story, Lukas's eyebrows lifted a little, his only reaction, while Cressida looked more and more horrified.

He remembered the chip in his pocket that Serena gave him before he left, and pulled it out. "She put all of her schematics on this if you want to know more," he said. "She said it's unencrypted."

Lukas accepted it. "Encryption wouldn't be a problem for me, anyway," he said wryly.

"Use my thincomp to read it," Cressida said.

Lukas rose from his seat and went to the bedroom, then returned with a battered thincomp held together with Super Seal. He pressed the chip against its cracked screen and gave it back to Matthias when the machine beeped. Lukas's eyes flitted back and forth faster than Matthias thought possible as he read the information there, reminding him again of what Lukas was.

He finally gave the thincomp to Cressida to read. "Colton Byers worked in a research capacity with the military's cyborg project," he said finally. "I remember his joining the research team after my second enhancement surgery. The cyborg project was financed by Caron Cybernetics, which dissolved after it was canceled."

"You knew him?" said Matthias excitedly.

"Tangentially," Lukas said. "Being a cyborg wasn't my choice, and I wasn't eager to make friends with the people who worked on me. But what happened to Serena is within the skill set of anyone who worked on that project and continued to do so after it was discontinued." His hands tightened into fists, and his next words had an undercurrent of rage to them. "It was illegal to continue cyborg experiments after me."

"This says Colton Byers bought her from her parents twelve years ago," Cressida said, looking up from the screen. "That's before you left the military."

"She's being polite," said Lukas to Matthias. "I went AWOL after I couldn't tolerate the abuse anymore."

Cressida gave him an exasperated look, but neither of them elaborated on his statement. "He must have continued his research after he was finished with you."

"The research team changed periodically," Lukas said. "Certain people worked in certain areas. The military didn't want everyone on the team to have a complete cyborg blueprint. Colton Byers took what he could and worked off that."

"Do you have any idea how to deactivate her nanobots so she isn't bound to a computer system?" Matthias asked.

Lukas paused, searching for words. Some of Matthias's excitement leached out of him.

"I think the easiest way to find that out is to go to the original source," he said. "She downloaded the entire history of her nanobots into this. We would have to go back to her moon compound and work from there. But," he continued, "I don't know if she can be permanently detached from a computer system."

Defeated, Matthias closed his eyes, already dreading telling Serena that bit of news.

"There's another but," Lukas said. "It's possible to make her nanobots automatically adaptable to other systems. She wouldn't be able to take a wilderness camping trip, but she could still live a relatively normal life, I think."

"So, she won't be stuck like this forever," Matthias translated. Some of his spirits buoyed.

"No, I don't think so. I'm also not a medic. I'm looking at this from a purely technical, cyborg point of view." To Cressida, he said, "Do you want to come with me to visit Serena?"

"You'll help us?" Matthias said.

"Of course," Lukas replied, looking a little affronted at the implication he wouldn't. "You'll need help at the moon compound, especially if Colton Byers is still there."

"I'll be honest with you," Matthias said. "I don't know how long we'll be gone."

"Let me pack a bag," Cressida said. She got up and went to the bedroom.

"You don't have work to worry about?" Matthias asked. "I'm not trying to sound ungrateful or talk you out of this, but ..."

"We're living off a settlement from MacQuarrie Galactic Tours at the moment," Lukas said.

"Which is great because I haven't picked up a new

employment contract yet, and we're still in the honeymoon phase," Cressida called from the bedroom.

Matthias thought he saw a slight blush color Lukas's face, but he couldn't be sure, and he wasn't about to needle the cyborg about it.

A few moments later, Cressida emerged from their bedroom, duffel in hand. Lukas took it from her and slung it over his shoulder. "Let's go," Lukas said.

For someone I designed to be so intelligent, she certainly took up with an idiot.

Colton chuckled a little to himself as he strode through the spaceport the *Ensign* was currently berthed in. What was Ericks thinking, moving his ship here? If he'd had a shred of sense, he would have left Echo-7 altogether.

No matter, he'd found the scow again easily enough.

Colton thanked the powers that be that there were so few moral citizens in Center City. The ease with which he'd been able to bribe a spaceport employee for access to the facility's security system was incredible. Colton moved in almost as soon as Matthias Ericks walked away from his secured ship.

But it was nothing that he couldn't breach now. And it was still early enough in the day that Serena would still be sleeping. She'd never been an early riser.

Keeping his head down in case she spotted him through a viewport, he approached the freighter's exterior door and pressed a modified descrambler stolen from the military to the palm lock. It whirred and clicked, erasing the authorized prints, and Colton pressed his hand to it.

The palm lock glowed green, and the rampway extended.

CHAPTER 14

A GREAT DEAL of Matthias's anxiety about Serena's situation had worn off when he, Lukas, and Cressida arrived at the spaceport. He didn't know until that point how helpless he'd felt, and for someone who was as independent and self-sufficient as he'd always been, that was a painful feeling to have.

But beside that pain resided something else, a deeper affection he harbored for Serena that he'd never had for anyone else.

While Lukas was still fairly reserved, Cressida was more open, asking him about Serena, his time in the military, his home planet, during the walk to the spaceport. Matthias answered, then had to ask some questions of his own that had been simmering in the back of his mind.

"How did you and Lukas meet?"

"Oh," she said. "That's related to our settlement from MacQuarrie. I guess you didn't hear about him when you were in the military?"

"I heard rumors about a cyborg project but kept myself out of the loop for a lot of things," Matthias replied. They passed the spaceport's security checkpoint and headed for the spaceport's landing pad. "I did the absolute bare minimum to keep me and my unit from being blown up to keep from being promoted since I was right on the frontlines on the Bravan border. I'm from Ixon, so I was conscripted," he explained.

"I was an experiment," Lukas said. "And I finally got sick of being experimented on and took my leave without asking. That's the short story of how we met."

Matthias might have asked for more clarification had the *Ensign* not come into view. He pressed his hand to the palm lock and the exterior door immediately opened, without the customary scan.

His breath caught. That wasn't supposed to happen. Had Serena been conducting repairs and accidentally deactivated the airlock's palm lock?

It was possible, but the chance was small. She would never make that kind of error.

"Oh, fuck," he said quietly.

"What is it?" Cressida asked from behind him.

Lukas replied before he could. "I don't think that's how secured airlock doors are supposed to work."

"No," said Matthias. He thought he might throw up.

The rampway automatically extended. Matthias, Lukas, and Cressida stepped on to it. Lukas turned around to face her. "Stay here," he said, handing her their duffel. "Give us a minute to check things out first."

She didn't argue, but clutched at the bag's strap and nodded.

"This isn't good," Matthias said as they walked through the ship.

He didn't have to have Serena's ability to know she wasn't on board. Even so, he still called, "Serena?"

"We're the only life forms on board," Lukas said, an unspoken apology in his voice.

"How can you tell?"

"Enhancements," the cyborg replied simply, and tapped at his temple. "Do you want to involve the authorities?"

"No, we're still not sure that Colton Byers isn't working with them."

"Good point. Would you have security visualizer footage available?"

"Yes." Matthias sagged against a bulkhead, feeling like he'd been turned inside out. His nausea had only intensified and the rest of him felt numb.

"Matthias." Lukas laid a hand on his arm, and despite all of what had happened, the gesture somehow kept Matthias from sliding to the floor in a boneless heap. "We're going to find her. I promise."

"Lukas?" Cressida called from the open airlock door. "Matthias? Is everything okay?"

"Give me a minute," Matthias said, voice rough. Lukas nodded and walked away.

When he'd collected himself enough to face them, he went back to the open airlock, where Lukas and Cressida waited, the latter looking anxious. "Security footage," Matthias said. "I can bring it up in the cockpit." He closed the airlock door.

It was a tight squeeze for two people in there, let alone three, but they still crowded around the forward viewscreen, where Matthias superimposed the exterior security footage from the visualizers. The only place he kept an interior visualizer was the airlock accessway, and he brought that up as well.

If Serena decided to take another stroll away from the ship...

But she hadn't. Matthias knew she hadn't. He'd spotted her fur wrap in the galley when he'd checked the rest of the *Ensign* while Lukas and Cressida waited. She wouldn't have left the ship without it.

A tall, well-built man with salt-and-pepper hair appeared on the screen, a small device in hand that he pressed against the *Ensign*'s palm lock. The exterior door opened without any resistance, and its ramp extended before he crept into the freighter's airlock. The interior visualizer picked up sound as well, and the intruder's boots didn't make a sound against the pitted metal deck.

The airlock was empty and silent for about six minutes until the man returned, a limp and silent Serena over his shoulder.

All three of them were silent for a few seconds, absorbing what they'd just seen.

Matthias was the first to speak. "God fucking damn it." He wanted to put his fist through something, just to take the edge off his rage, but remained still, staring at the viewscreen.

"Let's go to that moon," Lukas said. "Do you feel comfortable flying right now?"

"Yeah," said Matthias.

"Do you have weapons onboard?" Lukas asked. "I don't think this man is going to give her up without a fight." He held up his hands, encased in black gloves. "I have to get close to someone to fatally shock them."

Well, that was terrifying. "Yeah," Matthias repeated. "There's a weapons locker near the cargo bay. Two laser rifles and I keep them charged." His anger might even make him a better shot.

"All right," said Lukas. "Let's go."

***

Serena's body felt unnaturally heavy and unwieldy, and she fought to open her eyes. Was she sick? Her nanobots had never allowed her to get sick before.

When was the last time you were exposed to even a cold?

Something was off. The rumble of engines beneath her was unfamiliar—Matthias would have woken her up before leaving the spaceport—and she was lying on a sleeping pad that offered almost no comfort from the metal deck she lay on.

What the hell is going on?

She still couldn't keep her eyes open, and it took a few tries to get her voice to work. "Matthias?" Her voice was a croak. Maybe she'd managed to pick something up, after all.

"Not Matthias, Serena."

She immediately recognized the voice, and her blood ran cold. *No, no, no...!*

This had to be a bad dream. She was still aboard the *Ensign*, having a horrible nightmare, and any second she would wake up next to Matthias, and they could make love again and have breakfast, and then they would find that cyborg...

She struggled again, but as her body finally cooperated, she realized she was strapped into place. Her eyes finally focused, and she saw she was in a small one-person shuttle, fastened to the deck behind a pilot's seat. The back of a familiar head was in her view.

"Colton," she hissed.

"Good to see you, too," Colton replied, a false cheerfulness in his voice. Serena recognized that tone: it was the one he used when she'd managed to piss him off somehow and he was going to leave her alone on the compound long enough to make her panic. "Did you enjoy your little vacation?"

Serena stopped struggling enough to lean back and get a feel for the shuttle. She recognized it; it was Colton's personal craft.

"Serena?" he said, a little more sharply. "I asked you a question."

Her nanobots couldn't detect any flaws in the shuttle's design, nothing to use to her advantage. "Fuck you," she snarled.

Colton was silent for a moment. Probably shocked into silence, Serena figured. She'd never used that word in his presence before unless she counted writing it on the mirror in jam before she escaped SG-Paradise. She took advantage of the opportunity to struggle a little more against her bonds.

"You aren't getting loose," Colton said. "You're never getting loose ever again."

"Where are we going?" Serena demanded.

"Back home."

"How did you find me?"

"You don't get to ask questions anymore, Serena."

"The fuck I don't."

He finally spun around in his seat, his face a mask of rage. "How dare you?" he said. "How *dare* you run away after all I've done for you?"

"I didn't ask for any of this!" She tried to sit up again and failed. She stopped fighting against her bonds, wanting to conserve her energy for whatever lay ahead of them. "I didn't ask for my parents to sell me to you, I didn't ask for you to be turned into a cyborg, I didn't ask to be trapped on a moon for twelve years!" Her voice rose, and she screamed at him, "*Where are my parents?*"

Colton didn't answer that question, just swiveled back around to the shuttle's control panel. "We'll be back at the moon soon," he said. "I've adjusted your nanobots to function with the shuttle, but I'll have to tweak things a little once we get back. If you keep being difficult, I'll drug you again."

Serena stared at the back of his head.

How did I end up here? She remembered getting dressed after she kissed Matthias goodbye, and doing a little housekeeping in preparation for Lukas Best's visit. Not that there was much to clean: the *Ensign* was spare, and Matthias didn't have a lot of possessions. She'd made a cup of tea and had taken a sip as soon as she took it from the galley panel, and then she'd felt something cold press against the skin on the back of her neck...

Then everything went dark, and she woke up on Colton's shuttle.

"How did you find me?" she asked again.

He didn't answer right away, and she thought he might be giving her the silent treatment just to mess with her. Finally, he said, "You aren't as stealthy as you think."

Serena waited. She didn't want to give away any details of her escape. She'd rather he tell her what he already knew of Matthias and the *Ensign*.

"I was able to pick up enough of that scow's energy trail after it docked on the moon," he said. "It took a hell of a lot of time, but I did it, and it's easy enough to drug someone when they can't hear you behind them. I designed you to be smart, but I still created you."

Serena guessed that he didn't know Matthias had visited her more than once.

"How did you broadcast the location beacon without me finding out?" Colton demanded.

I didn't. Matthias's navigation system was thrown offline and it picked it up accidentally. He never would have Serena if that hadn't happened. She didn't dare voice her knowledge.

"You're smarter than I am," she said. "You tell me."

Colton slammed his hands on the control panel. "This new attitude of yours ..." He turned around again to face her. "It ends now."

"It doesn't."

"It does." He leaned down from his seat, a smirk forming on his lips. "You're forgetting who designed those nanobots and knows just what they can do. As far as you're concerned, I'm your god."

Fear slammed into Serena, replacing her anger and frustration.

Nanobots controlled her brain functions.

He could control how she felt, how she reacted if he wanted to. The full import of his words finally sunk in. She wouldn't be her own person anymore, just a plaything encased in human flesh if Colton desired.

She forced herself to breathe, to remain calm, but a couple of tears still slipped down her cheeks.

"I hope you'll see things my way," Colton said.

Serena turned her head away to face the opposite wall and hoped Matthias would find her soon.

Serena didn't know what Colton had drugged her with, nor was she sure how much time had passed, but she drifted in and out of consciousness through the shuttle journey. She didn't ask any more questions, and Colton wasn't forthcoming with any information, so she stayed quiet and faced the wall opposite him.

She tried to formulate a plan. If they were returning to the moon compound, she could find a way to escape again. SG-Paradise was the likeliest place they were headed to, given the equipment there and her nanobots' attachment to it. She would be in familiar territory.

She would be obedient and meek and make a move when Colton had his guard down. She would have to find a way to get another SOS out, maybe even broadcast it across the galaxy.

Matthias had to be so worried.

She loved him so much, and she hated that he would have to go through this ordeal again. She dearly hoped he'd managed to make contact with Lukas Best, that the cyborg would have more answers.

But if he didn't...

She steeled her reserve. She'd lived through this and managed to escape, and she could do it again, with Matthias or without him.

The shuttle's engines shut off, and she heard Colton stand up. He moved silently through the shuttle's cockpit, and when she looked, she saw the soles of his boots were wrapped in rubberized felt. That must have been how he'd managed to sneak up on her in the *Ensign*'s galley.

She didn't move as he unfastened her straps, nor when his hand needlessly grazed over her breast, which he'd never done before. She suppressed a shudder. "Get up," he ordered her.

She stood up on wobbly legs, grabbing the back of the pilot's seat for balance. "Move," he said.

The shuttle's ramp extended, and she saw the familiar, hated sight of the moon compound's docking bay stretched out before her.

And Matthias still had the moon's coordinates. She'd made sure of that when she made that chip with her diagnostics. Colton could erase a location beacon's coordinates from the public record, make it unsearchable, but the beacon itself would still exist. She relaxed a little.

She wrapped her arms around herself to guard against the chill as Colton marched her through the hangar, back to her apartment.

"So, Serena," he finally said. "This will never happen again."

"You keep saying that." She stared daggers at him. "Could you please tell me what happened to my parents?"

"In all your romping around the Zone, you never found out?"

"No."

Colton shrugged off his flight jacket and carelessly tossed it on the couch. "Do you really want to know?"

"That's why I keep asking. Why did they sell me to you? What did you offer them?"

Colton crossed the room to the kitchen area. "Would you like some tea?"

She had to force herself to remain calm. "No, thank you. But I *would* like to finally know what happened to my parents."

"You're going to hate me if I tell you," he said. Then, a little quieter, "For a while, anyway."

Serena remembered what he'd said about his controlling her nanobots, and a shudder rippled through her.

He's going to reprogram me.

But she waited. This might be the only opportunity she would ever get to find out what happened to them.

"Your parents started using darfin," Colton said. He set some water to boil. "Your father also had a gambling habit."

Serena remembered her parents being distant and chilly, but she'd always chalked that up to being constantly stressed about their lives in a very expensive part of the Zone, and the pressure of raising a kid in that environment. "I didn't know they used darfin," she said. "I don't remember them ever showing the signs." They'd lived in Center City's suburbs. The suburbs weren't supposed to have drug problems.

"The darfin we think of now didn't exist until a few years ago," Colton said. "Much stronger, more addictive strains hit the Zone around the time your parents turned you over to me. It was more expensive then, too.

"Anyway, the military's cyborg project was scaled back, and a lot of researchers were reassigned to other developments," Colton said. "I wasn't ready to give up the research, and I still believe an enhanced military is the future. It's been completely shut down on the official channels."

"But you're still experimenting," Serena said.

"I've been comparing my experiments and results with

Garrett," Colton said, referring to that mysterious friend of his whom Serena had never met. "You're a valuable commodity. I have people interested in seeing what exactly an enhanced person can do. Cyborgs without any physical indicators of their enhancements, who are bound to a specific location to survive—there are a lot of industries out there that can use that kind of labor."

"You're talking about slavery."

Once again, Colton waved his hand as if to dismiss her concerns.

Serena sidestepped that newly revealed bit of information, as much as she was loathe to. "My parents," she said, trying to steer the conversation back to where she wanted it. "What happened to them? Did you keep track of them after they sold me to you?"

"Thirty thousand scrip buys a lot of darfin," Colton said.

"Colton, *please*," she said, hating the whiny note in her voice.

"They're dead, Serena." He pinned her with a hard stare. "I couldn't take the risk that they'd sober up and change their minds about selling you. I killed them."

CHAPTER 15

MATTHIAS SET a course for the moon's hidden coordinates, then stared at the forward viewscreen. *Paradise. What a fucked-up thing to name it.*

"Are you sure you don't want me to take over?" Lukas asked from the co-pilot's seat.

"It's a straight run on the edge of Zone space," Matthias said. "No subspace exits to worry about, not that this boat can handle subspace."

"She hasn't been outfitted with subspace engines?" Lukas asked.

He was trying to keep Matthias's mind off Serena and what they faced once they reached the moon compound, assuming she was there. "No," Matthias said. "There's no point since the war's kept me from moving between the Zone and Brava System. I can do all the work I need to just trawling through the space lanes the regular way. God damn it," he said, gripping the edge of the control screen. His voice cracked. "Sorry, it's not you."

"I know," Lukas said. "Believe me, I know." He glanced down at the co-pilot's controls, where the *Ensign*'s course was plotted out before him. "You never did tell me how you found out who I am and where I was. How you found Valenna."

"Serena did it," Matthias said. "I told you about her ability to integrate herself with computer systems. She could do it with the galactic net."

Lukas nodded. "There's no escaping it, is there?"

"I don't know about that," Matthias replied, thinking of Serena's parents. And Serena herself. "There are certainly ways to make someone disappear from the public record. Serena found a bounty hunter who gave us your name, which eventually led to Valenna's address, although we were led to believe it was yours."

"Fucking Dalton!" Cressida snapped from her spot behind them. "It must've been Dalton!"

Lukas's expression darkened at the mention of Janek Dalton's name, too. "How much did it set you back to get my name?" he asked.

"Couple thousand scrip." Based on Lukas and Cressida's reactions, he didn't press them on their relationship to the bounty hunter. But there was one thing he was curious about. "Why did you give Valenna your old apartment? That was generous of you."

Was it possible Lukas could get angrier? Matthias immediately regretted asking the question.

"We needed to move," Cressida said. "Originally, it was because we didn't want Valenna to know our address, and we needed a bigger place, but she went to rehab, and she's making an effort to get her life together and needed somewhere to stay. There were a few months left on the lease and it was cheaper for her than renting elsewhere."

"For now," Lukas said. "She's trying to get her life together *for now*."

"This is the longest she's stayed sober," Cressida said.

"And we haven't completely forgiven her for everything yet, but she's family."

"Valenna and Dalton are well acquainted," Lukas said.

Damn it. Matthias made a note never to ask either of them about Dalton or Valenna again. But at least Valenna was trying to create a better life for herself, and she had Cressida's support, albeit grudgingly.

Lukas changed the subject. "Want to show me that weapons locker?"

"Yeah." It was best that they be prepared for everything once they arrived at the compound. Matthias knew Colton wouldn't give up Serena without a fight.

"I'll stay here," Cressida said and took Lukas's place in the co-pilot's seat.

Matthias led Lukas to his weapons locker, not that he had much. Lukas removed one of the rifles hanging there and hefted it, then peered down its scope. "Not exactly military-grade."

"Yeah, well, I had enough military-grade weaponry to last me a lifetime when I was still enlisted." He checked the charge on the other one. It glowed green, at full power.

"I hear you on that." Lukas replaced the rifle. "They'll still do some serious damage if it comes to that."

"As long as Serena stays out of the crossfire." Matthias put the other one away and closed the locker.

Lukas regarded him thoughtfully.

"I love her," Matthias said.

The cyborg's expression didn't change. "I hear you on that, too."

"I haven't told her yet."

"Well," Lukas said, "We'd better get to that moon so you can."

Serena had retreated to her old bedroom without a word of complaint from Colton. He'd removed the door since she left so she didn't have any privacy, but at least he didn't follow her in.

The mirror was smashed to pieces, though. Plastiglas shards, some with her taunting goodbye message written on them, were spread across the dresser. She paced the room, trying to figure out her next move.

She'd tried to log into the compound's computers but found that Colton managed to lock her and her nanobots out for the first time ever. Her modified thincomp, like all of her most treasured belongings, had been left behind on the *Ensign*. She couldn't feel the compound's life support thrumming around her, nor pick up any passing ships.

This is what life would be like without my nanobots.

It was jarring, and given her current circumstances, terrifying. She'd wanted to be free of the nanobots but on her terms.

She walked toward the bedroom's doorway, movements jerky.

What the …? She hadn't meant to do that.

She fought against it, to stay in her room, but she was compelled to move forward, half-stomping back to the apartment's main area.

Colton waited, settled into a chair, his thincomp on his lap. "Sit down," he said.

"No." But she kept on walking until she plunked heavily on the chair opposite him.

Panic clawed at her, as the realization of what Colton had just done hit her.

"My control over your nanobots will increase until you listen to me," Colton said. "If you still want to keep some of your free will, you'll behave. Do you get it?"

Tears pricked at her eyes, and she angrily brushed them away. At least she could still control her hands.

And he would take that away if she didn't cooperate. She nodded.

"Put some dinner together," Colton said. "And tell me all about how you managed to escape."

"Don't you already know?"

"I'd like to hear it from you."

Serena's mind raced, thinking about what to do next. She got to her feet and walked the short distance to the kitchen nook. She took her time perusing the ready-meals in the cupboards.

"Steak sounds good," she said uselessly. "Do you want that?"

Steak needed to be cut with knives. Especially the rubbery crap Colton supplied her with.

"Steak sounds fine," Colton said. "Now, tell me how you escaped."

Serena stuck two steak dinners in the food processor. She took out a tray and arranged cutlery on it. "I hacked the compound's system," she said. "I was able to get a distress signal out, and Matthias responded."

The processor pinged, and Serena put the dinners on the tray.

"And he helped you, just like that?" Suspicion dripped from Colton's voice.

Serena returned to the living area with the tray and sat down, setting it on a table between them. "Well, I fucked him."

Her crude words had their desired effect. Colton looked at her in shock, and she took advantage of the opportunity to plunge one of the knives between his ribs.

He'd designed her to be faster and stronger than the

average human woman, and she was going to use those enhancements to save herself.

He didn't relinquish his grip on the thincomp as she'd hoped. For a heart-stopping second, she thought she missed and just stabbed through a layer of clothes or a laser-proofed vest, some kind of protection she didn't know he had.

But he let out a guttural roar of pain. "You bitch!"

Serena reached for his thincomp, but he swatted her hand away and tapped at its screen with shaking fingers. The device slid to the floor, and he reached for his side where the knife protruded.

"God damn it," he said, his voice rough and raspy. "I think you hit my lung."

The full import of what she'd just done, that she was capable of doing such a thing, hit her. Her chest constricted and tears flowed down her cheeks. She couldn't tell if she was rooted in place because of shock or something he'd done to her nanobots.

Colton staggered to his feet and reached for the knife. Agony painted across his face, he pulled it out and dropped it on the floor. He pressed his hand to the wound, but it did nothing to staunch the blood flow.

She had never seen so much before. She swallowed in an attempt to keep nausea at bay.

"That was a stupid move on your part," he wheezed. He collapsed back on the chair, legs akimbo, hand still at his side.

As if on cue, the apartment's lights flickered.

Serena finally found her voice. "What did you do?"

"I shut it all down," Colton said. There was a pained grimace on his face, and she realized he was trying to smile. "You've killed us both."

The lights brightened for a few seconds, and just as quickly they turned off, and the apartment was plunged into darkness.

The only light source was that of the thincomp screen, and she moved for it. At least her immobility was caused by shock instead of Colton's machinations. "What's going on?" she asked, hating the wobble in her voice.

"You fucking stabbed me," Colton said. His voice was quieter now. "And I'm bleeding to death. You hit something vital, you bitch." He coughed, a thick, wet sound.

Serena picked up the thincomp, now on lockout mode. She pressed at it, trying to make it work, but it remained frozen.

"This is it," said Colton. "For both of us." He coughed again. "The life support will start failing soon."

She held the thincomp in her hands, trying to connect with it, feel out which functions had been tampered with. But she may as well have been holding a tea cube in her hands.

"Your nanobots will start failing soon, too," Colton said. His voice was breathier now, and he must have moved his hand because Serena heard the squish of sodden fabric. She blinked back another wave of tears.

Using the thincomp screen's light to see by, she checked every machine in the apartment, trying desperately to pick up a signal. But she couldn't sense anything, and the chill from deep space was already creeping into the compound. She returned to her bedroom to put on some more clothes and boots.

The living area was silent when she returned. Colton's wet, raspy breath had ceased.

"Colton?" she whispered. Still using the thincomp's glow, she checked on him.

His face was slack, and dark blood stained his clothes and the chair. She tentatively reached out and shook his shoulder. "Colton?"

His head lolled to the side.

Serena began to shake. She dropped the thincomp, but it didn't fall to the floor. Instead, it floated away.

So did she. So did Colton, body rising from the chair like a summoned ghoul from a horror vid.

The gravity functions were deactivated. Soon the air would cycle down and she would suffocate.

She screamed at the unwelcome feeling of weightlessness, at her own frustration, at the reality that she'd condemned herself to die with Colton. The thincomp floated by her, and its illumination revealed her angry tears balled up into tiny spheres drifting away from her face.

Colton's body pushed into her, heavy and bloody. She kicked him away and swam through the air as far as she could.

The air.

How long did she have before she ran out of air?

She bumped into one of the windows that revealed the desolate, bare moon the compound rested on, the only view she'd ever had from here.

Even if Matthias was on his way to rescue her again, she'd be dead before he could get here.

She dragged her hand over her eyes, pushing spherical tears away from her face.

I love him so much, and I never told him.

CHAPTER 16

THE MOON COMPOUND was completely dark. Had he not had the location beacon or coordinates, Matthias would have missed it.

They weren't there.

"God damn it," Matthias said. He opened a hail, but a response didn't come, just the crackle of deep space static. It was like the compound didn't exist anymore.

Lukas sat in the co-pilot's seat, watching everything Matthias was doing on the screen there. "Its power grid is totally shut off," he said. "Its life support is offline, too. It's completely abandoned."

That didn't sound right. It was one thing to turn off the lights, quite another to deactivate a compound's entire power supply. "I still want to check it out," Matthias said.

"I understand. Do you have an EVA suit?"

"Yeah." He'd never had to conduct an emergency exterior repair while in the space lanes, but it was better to have the suit and not need it, then need it and not have it. "Will you and Cressida be okay onboard?"

Lukas gave him the closest thing to an incredulous look that Matthias thought he could muster.

"Can you handle the ship while I force the docking bay open?" Matthias asked.

There was that look again.

"Do you have the equipment to do that?" the cyborg asked.

"Yeah. The bay's sealed off from the living area, and I don't want to take any chances if she's still in there." His stomach turned over at the thought that she might be trapped on that compound. Trapped, or worse.

"And even if they aren't there," he continued, "There could be evidence of where they've gone."

He was already up and headed for the airlock accessway, where his EVA suit waited in a closet, along with a tool kit. He put on the suit, and Lukas double-checked its seals and pronounced it safe. "Is there a comm in there?" he asked.

Matthias activated it. "Yeah. I'll manually connect the door breaker to the bay, and you can activate it from the cockpit."

"Good. If anything feels off, or you're not comfortable in the suit, let me know, and I'll bring you back in."

Lukas left the airlock and sealed the interior door from the accessway. Matthias opened the exterior door and stepped out into open space, magnetized boots latching themselves to the bay door.

"How are you?" Lukas asked.

Matthias fitted a door breaker in the tiny space between the doors and activated it. "Still alive." The readout on the inside of his helmet told him his air supply was at one hundred percent. "You should be able to connect to the breaker now," he said.

"Just a minute."

"Everything okay on your end?"

There was a heart-stopping pause before Lukas said,

"There's a life form in the compound. Are you *sure* the bay is separated from the living quarters?"

"Serena," Matthias whispered.

"Definitely human, definitely alive," said Lukas. "But life support has failed. I don't know how much air she has."

"Can you try hailing the compound?"

"I can't," said Lukas gently. "You're going to have to take a chance and go in there."

He didn't have a choice in the matter. Matthias closed his eyes and hoped he wasn't about to make the biggest mistake of his life.

"Okay," he said. "Force open the doors."

There was a darkened shuttle in the bay, its doors sealed. Someone still had to be in the compound.

The door dividing the bay from the control room and corridor to the apartment was still sealed. Matthias uttered a quick prayer of thanks before prying it away, taking care to close and manually seal it behind him, and he now noticed that he felt lighter, more buoyant despite wearing magnetized boots. The gravity had been shut off. He half-walked down the short corridor to the apartment's entrance, an involuntary bounce in his step, the light on his EVA helmet the only illumination.

An airtight plastiglas door led to the apartment itself, and his head lamp's light bounced off the floor. Objects floated past, and something hit the plastiglas, obstructing his view. It turned around, and Matthias found himself face-to-face with a dead man. His eyes were wide open, pupils rolled back in his head.

If his boots hadn't been bound to the floor, he would have jumped back. As it was, a yelp escaped him.

"Matthias?" said Lukas.

"There's a dead guy here," Matthias said.

"There's someone alive there, too," Lukas said.

He raised his head, trying to shine the suit's lamp in the room.

A familiar dark-haired woman, bundled up in sweaters and scarves, floated to the door. Her face was tear-streaked, her hands reaching out to the door, and Matthias had never seen a better sight in his life.

He hardly dared to believe what he was seeing.

She clawed at the door until she managed to get it open. Matthias grabbed her hands to keep her from floating away.

Her voice sounded far away through his helmet, even though she was right in front of him and he would never let her go again. "You found me," she said between sobs. Her tears collected in balls under her eyes and floated away.

"I said I would." He had to raise his voice to make sure she could hear it. "Do you have an EVA suit? We need to get out of here."

"Colton's shuttle is here," she said. "There'll probably be one in there." A sob escaped her as she looked behind her at the body. "He's dead."

He squeezed her hands, wishing he could feel more through his gloves. "What happened?"

She didn't reply, only looked away. He'd wait before asking about him again. "I'll get it, and we'll get you out of here," he offered.

"We?"

"Lukas Best and Cressida Merchant are here," Matthias said. "They helped me get the docking bay open."

Serena's hair floated around her as she nodded, but he could tell she wasn't focusing on Lukas anymore. "I killed him," she said. "He tried to adjust my nanobots so I would have to obey him, and I killed him." She clung to Matthias and squeezed her eyes shut. "I wasn't thinking, I just reacted."

Revulsion coursed through Matthias at her words, when he thought about what Colton had done and tried to do to her. She needed to get away from this place. "Serena," he said urgently. "I'll go to the shuttle and find the EVA suit, and I'll be back in a couple of minutes. There isn't any life support in the bay, no air, nothing. Can you wait that long?"

She nodded. "Please hurry."

Matthias hated to let her go again, but he did, closing the plastiglas door behind him. With bouncing footsteps, he walked back to the hangar.

Serena hated that she had was forced to use Colton's EVA suit to get away from the compound, but it was her only way out. The locked thincomp in hand, she followed Matthias out of her old prison, through pitch-black corridors to the waiting *Ensign*.

But she held it together long enough to get on board, the airlock door securely sealed behind them. She stripped off the bulky, too-large suit as soon as she could.

Matthias did the same, and he immediately pulled her to him in a warm hug.

"I killed him," she repeated.

"It's okay."

"I wasn't thinking. I just didn't want to be a zombie. That's what he wanted to turn me into." she said into his chest. Colton's thincomp was wedged between them. "I can't get this to work. I can't sense it."

She couldn't sense anything on the *Ensign*, either. She felt the engines' thrum under her feet, but that was it.

"We'll see if Lukas can't help us out," Matthias said.

She pulled away from him enough to drag her sleeve over her eyes. The concern in his gaze made her feel a little more stable, and she breathed deeply, trying to center herself.

He kissed her, and she eagerly leaned into him, needing to be as close to him as she could be.

"I love you," she said. "All I could think while I was in there was that I was going to suffocate and I wouldn't get a chance to tell you."

"I love you, too," he said. "Although I did tell Lukas about that before you."

She managed a small laugh at that.

"Come on," he said. "Let's get away from this place and see what Lukas can do with Colton's thincomp."

Lukas and Cressida were waiting for them in the corridor outside the airlock accessway. Matthias made quick work of the introductions, then asked Lukas to take a look at the thincomp.

Lukas peered at the device's ports and exterior sensors, then patted his trouser pockets, coming up with a connector. "Is there somewhere I can sit down and plug into this?" he asked.

"The galley," Matthias said. "It'll have enough room for everyone."

They crowded into the galley, and Serena watched in fascination as Lukas connected himself to the thincomp through a port in his wrist. There was another one in his neck. "I can usually do that myself with my nanobots," she said. "But I can't anymore."

The thincomp's error screen cleared. Lukas handed it back to Serena.

She stared at it for a moment. She finally had access to all of Colton's secrets.

The first thing she had to do was find out how her

nanobots worked. She opened a file with her name on it and began reading.

He could control her nanobots' function and her whole life with a few taps of his fingers. She noted the settings and responses he'd started programming, the file changes dated in the days before he'd brought her back to the compound. He had intended to turn her into a subservient, mindless doll following her return, determined to stamp out any trace of her personality. She saw a graph of her movements and biological functions as they worked in tandem with her nanobots, right up until she stabbed Colton.

Or just before. She blinked, trying to make more sense of what she was reading. Maybe she was wrong.

"Lukas, could you take a look at this?" She handed the thincomp to him.

His eyes scanned over the screen with inhuman speed. "He completely shut off your nanobots," he said. "According to this program, he had to do that to make any adjustments to their function. He was the only person in the universe who could do that."

Serena stared at him for a second, then to Matthias, who wore a hopeful expression.

"My nanobots are turned off," she said.

"I'd do a diagnostic in the sickbay, but according to this, they are." A smile tugged at the corners of his mouth. "He was trying to do the cyborg equivalent of a total re-do when he did this, re-programming your nanobots from the ground up."

"I'm not bound to the compound or the *Ensign*."

Lukas shook his head.

Serena turned around and ran for the sickbay, Matthias just behind her.

She was free.

She couldn't sense a damn thing in the sickbay when she touched the equipment. It was scary to lose that, but it meant she was normal. She lay on the diag bed and waited while Matthias set the machine to run a body scan.

She didn't know she was holding her breath until Matthias looked up from the readout, a smile on his face. "They're deactivated," he said. "Everything else is functioning as it should. Your muscles, your respiratory system, everything."

"My heart," she said.

She climbed off the bed and wrapped her arms around Matthias, the best place in the galaxy to be.

EPILOGUE

ACCORDING to the voluminous data contained on Colton's thincomp, there didn't appear to be any other nanobot-enhanced cyborgs in the Zone. It was a short-lived relief since Serena and the data reminded Matthias of Colton's friend Garrett Jacoby, fellow cyborg researcher who was still at large.

Despite the deactivated nanobots, no one was able to breathe until the *Ensign* left the compound and Serena's condition remained unchanged. Matthias figured it would take a long time for either of them to stop being nervous about her nanobots.

They returned to Echo-7 long enough to leave Lukas and Cressida in Center City, with promises to remain in touch. Matthias, who was usually bad at doing that, knew he would hold his end of the bargain. He knew he could never repay them for their help.

Serena hadn't been interested in exploring Center City, instead enthusiastically agreeing to a trip to Ixon. "Are you sure?" he'd asked her. "My mother's there."

"I'd like to meet her." She leaned back in the co-pilot's seat, a smile across her face. "She must be nice. She seems nice when you two talk. She raised you, after all."

That was how they found themselves disembarking from the *Ensign* during a blizzard, then waiting for a shuttle to take them to his mother's home, an antigrav pallet behind them carrying some much-needed supplies.

Grace threw open the door. "You told me Serena's just your friend," she said by way of greeting.

"There are all different kinds of friends, Mom," he said, leaning down to kiss her cheek. "And right now, my friend's freezing her ass off. Let us in."

Grace stepped out of the way to let them in, and they shook the snow off their parkas in the foyer. "I'm pleased to see she's a *different* kind of friend to you," she said. "I like the look of her." She held out her hand to Serena. "It's nice to meet you in person."Serena shook it, and Grace took advantage of it to pull her in a hug, which Serena returned.

Grace let go of Serena and took a couple of steps back to look at them. "You two look good together," she said. "And I made cookies. Take your boots off and you can have some in the kitchen." She turned around and walked down the hall. "And you'll have to tell me all about how you met," she added over her shoulder. "I'm sure there's more to the story than Antonoff Station."

"I'd like to say she's not always like this, but she is," Matthias murmured as they toed off their boots.

"I like her already."

"She likes you, too." He lightly kissed her, mindful of Grace returning and saying something. "But not as much as I love you."

Serena's gaze was intense enough that he considered leaving and taking her back to their cabin on the *Ensign*. "I love you, too."

Matthias squeezed her hand and led her down the hall. "Well, Mom," he said. "It's an interesting story."

ABOUT THE AUTHOR

Jessica Marting is a sci-fi and paranormal romance author, art enthusiast (not quite an artist, despite all that time in art school), an avid reader, and makeup collector. She lives in Toronto.

Sign up for her newsletter at jessicamarting.com/newsletter for pre-order alerts, sales, freebies, and more.

Magic & Mechanicals

Wolf's Lady

Sea Change

Bound in Blood

Dragon's Keep

Zone Cyborgs

Haven

Paradise

Oasis

Safe Harbor

Sanctuary

Refuge

The Commons

Supernova

Celestial Chaos

Standalone Novels & Novellas

Spindle's End

Trade Secrets

Neon Vice

Dead Ringer

Escape From Europa 10

Castaways

Demon's Favor